𝓟

Kid Wolf of Texas

**Center Point
Large Print**

**This Large Print Book carries the
Seal of Approval of N.A.V.H.**

Kid Wolf of Texas

PAUL S. POWERS

CENTER POINT PUBLISHING
THORNDIKE, MAINE

This Center Point Large Print edition
is published in the year 2006 by arrangement with
Golden West Literary Agency.

Copyright © 1930 by Paul S. Powers.
Copyright © renewed 1958 by Paul S. Powers.

All rights reserved.

The text of this Large Print edition is unabridged. In other
aspects, this book may vary from the original edition. Printed in
Thailand. Set in 16-point Times New Roman type.

ISBN 1-58547-712-5

Library of Congress Cataloging-in-Publication Data

Powers, Paul S. (Paul Sylvester), 1905-1971.
  Kid Wolf of Texas / Paul S. Powers.--Center Point large print ed.
    p. cm.
  ISBN 1-58547-712-5 (lib. bdg. : alk. paper)
    1. Large type books. I. Title.

PS3531.O9725K53 2006
813'.52--dc22
                                                        2005022528

CONTENTS

CONTENTS

CHAPTER I

THE LIVING DEAD

"Oh, I want to go back to the Rio Grande!
    The Rio!
    That's where I long to be!"

T he words, sung in a soft and musical tenor, died
away and changed to a plaintive whistle, leaving
the scene more lonely than ever. For a few moments
nothing was to be seen except the endless expanse of
wilderness, and nothing was to be heard save the
mournful warble of the singer. Then a horse and rider
were suddenly framed where the sparse timber opened
out upon the plain.

Together, man and mount made a striking picture; yet
it would have been hard to say which was the more picturesque—the rider or the horse. The latter was a
splendid beast, and its spotless hide of snowy white
glowed in the rays of the afternoon sun. With bit chains
jingling, it gracefully leaped a gully, landing with all the
agility of a mountain lion, in spite of its enormous size.

The rider, still whistling his Texas tune, swung in the
concha-decorated California stock saddle as if he were
a part of his horse. He was a lithe young figure, dressed
in fringed buckskin, touched here and there with the
gay colors of the Southwest and of Mexico.

Two six-guns, wooden-handled, were suspended

7

from a cartridge belt of carved leather, and hung low on each hip. His even teeth showed white against the deep sunburn of his face.

"Reckon we-all bettah cut south, Blizzahd," he murmured to his horse. "We haven't got any business on the Llano."

He spoke in the soft accents of the old South, and yet his speech was colored with just a trace of Spanish—a musical drawl seldom heard far from that portion of Texas bordering the Rio Bravo del Norte.

Wheeling his mount, he searched the landscape with his keen blue eyes. Behind him was broken country; ahead of him was the terrible land that men have called the Llano Estacado. The land rose to it in a long series of steppes with sharp ridges.

Queerly shaped and oddly colored buttes ascended toward it in a puzzling tangle. Dim in the distance was the Llano itself—a mesa with a floor as even as a table; a treeless plain without even a weed or shrub for a landmark; a plateau of peril without end.

The rider was doing well to avoid the Llano Estacado. Outlaw Indian bands roamed over its desolate expanse—the only human beings who could live there. In the winter, snowstorms raced screaming across it, from Texas to New Mexico, for half a thousand miles. It was a country of extremes. In the summer it was a scorching griddle of heat dried out by dry desert winds. Water was hard to find there, and food still harder to obtain. And it was now late summer—the season of mocking mirages and deadly sun.

The horseman was just about to turn his steed's head directly to the southward when a sound came to his ears—a cry that made his eyes widen with horror.

Few sounds are so thrillingly terrible as the dying scream of a mangled horse, and yet this was far more awful. Only the throat of a human being could emit that chilling cry. It rose in shrill crescendo, to die away in a sobbing wail that lifted the hair on the listener's head. Again and again it came—a moan born of the frightful torture of mortal agony.

Giving his mount a touch of spur, the horseman turned the animal westward toward the Llano Estacado. So horrible were the sounds that he had paled under his tan. But he headed directly toward the direction of the cries. He knew that some human being was suffering frightful pain.

Crossing a sun-baked gully, he climbed upward and onto a flat-topped, miniature butte. Here he saw a spectacle that literally froze him with horror.

Although accustomed to a hundred gruesome sights in that savage land, he had never seen one like this. Staked on the ground, feet and arms wide-stretched, and securely bound, was a man. Or rather, it was a thing that had once been a man. It was a torture that even the diabolical mind of an Indian could not have invented. It was the insane creation of another race—the work of a madman.

For the suffering wretch had been left on his back, face up to the sun, with his eyelids removed!

Ants crawled over the sufferer, apparently believing

him dead. Flies buzzed, and a raven flapped away, heating the air with its startled wings. The horseman dismounted, took his water bag from his horse, and approached the tortured man.

The moaning man on the ground did not see him, for his eyes were shriveled. He was blind.

The youth with the water bag tried to speak, but at first words failed to come. The sight was too ghastly.

"Heah's watah," he muttered finally. "Just—just try and stand the pain fo' a little longah. I'll do all I can fo' yo'."

He held the water bag at the swollen, blackened lips. Then he poured a generous portion of the contents over the shriveled eyes and skeletonlike face.

For a while the tortured man could not speak. But while his rescuer slashed loose the rawhide ropes that bound him, he began to stammer a few words:

"Heaven bless yuh! I thought I was dead, or mad! Oh, how I wanted water! Give me more—more!"

"In a little while," said the other gently.

In spite of the fact that he was now free, the sufferer could not move his limbs. Groans came from his lips.

"Shoot me!" he cried. "Put a bullet through me! End this, if yuh've got any pity for me! I'm blind—dying. I can't stand the pain. Yuh must have a gun. Why don't yuh kill me and finish me?"

It was the living dead! The buckskin-clad youth gave him more water, his face drawn with compassion.

"Yo'll feel bettah afta while," he murmured. "Just sit steady."

"Too late!" the tortured man almost screamed. "I'm dyin', I tell yuh!"

"How long have yo' been like this?"

"Three-four days. Maybe five. I lost count."

"Who did this thing?" was the fierce question.

"'The Terror'!" the reply came in a sobbing wail. "'The Masked Terror' and his murderin' band. I was a prospector. A wagon train was startin' across the Llano, and I tried to warn 'em. I never reached 'em. The Terror cut me off and left me like this! Say, I don't know yore name, pard, but—"

"Call me 'Kid Wolf,'" answered the youth, "from Texas." His eyes had narrowed at the mention of the name "The Terror."

"Somethin' on my mind, Kid Wolf. It's that wagon train. The Terror will wipe it out. Promise me yuh'll try and warn 'em."

"I promise, old-timah," murmured the Texan. "Only yo' needn't to have asked that. When yo' first mentioned it, I intended to do it. Where is this wagon train, sah?"

In gasps—for his strength was rapidly failing him—the prospector gave what directions he could. Kid Wolf listened intently, his eyes blazing-blue coals.

"I'm passin' in my checks," sighed the sufferer weakly, when he had given what information he could. "I'll go easier now."

"Yo' can be sure that I'll do all I can," the Texan assured him. "Fo' yo' see, that's always been mah business. I'm just a soldier of misfohtune, goin' through life tryin' to do all I can fo' the weak and oppressed. I'll risk mah life fo' these people, and heah's mah hand on that!"

The prospector groped for his hand, took it, and tried to smile. In a few moments he had breathed his last, released from his pain. Kid Wolf removed the bandanna from his own throat and placed it over the dead man's face. Then he weighted it down with small rocks and turned to go.

"Just about the time I get to thinkin' the world is good, Blizzahd," he sighed, addressing his white horse, "I find somethin' like this. Well, seems like we hit out across the Llano, aftah all. Let's get a move on, amigo! We've got work to do."

The Texan's face, as he swung himself into the saddle, was set and hard.

"Oh, I'm goin' back to the Rio Grande!
    The Rio!
  For most a yeah, I've been away,
And I'm lonesome now fo' me Old Lone Stah!
    The Rio!
  Wheah the gila monsters play!"

It was Kid Wolf's second day on the Llano Estacado, and his usual good spirits had returned. His voice rose tunefully and cheerily above the steady drumming of Blizzard's hoofs.

Surely the scene that lay before his eyes could not have aroused his enthusiasm. It was lonely and desolate enough, with its endless sweeps dim against each horizon. The sky, blue, hot and pitiless, came down to meet the land on every hand, making a great circle unbroken by hill or mountain.

So clean-swept was the floor of the vast table-land that each mile looked exactly like another mile. There was not a tree, not a shrub, not a rock to break the weary monotony. It was no wonder that the Spanish padres, who had crossed this enormous plateau long before, had named it the Llano Estacado—the Staked Plains. They had had a good reason of their own. In order to keep the trail marked, they had been compelled to drive stakes in the ground as they went along. Although the stakes had gone long since, the name still stuck.

The day before, the Texan had climbed the natural rock steps that led upward and westward toward the terrible mesa itself, each flat-topped table bringing him nearer the Staked Plains. And soon after reaching the plateau he had found the trail left by a wagon train.

From the ruts left in the soil, Kid Wolf estimated that the outfit must consist of a large number of prairie schooners, atleast twenty. The Texan puzzled his mind over why this wagon train was taking such a dangerous route. Where were they bound for? Surely for the Spanish settlements of New Mexico—a perilous venture, at best.

Even on the level plain, a wagon outfit moves slowly, and the Texan gained rapidly. Hourly the signs he had been following grew fresher. Late in the afternoon he made out a blot on the western horizon—a blot with a hazy smudge above it. It was the wagon train. The smudge was dust, dug up by the feet of many oxen.

"They must be loco," Kid Wolf muttered, "to try and cut across The Terror's territory."

The Texan had heard much of The Terror. And what plainsman of that day hadn't? He was the scourge of the table-lands, with his band of a hundred cutthroats, desperadoes recruited from the worst scum of the border. More than half of his hired killers, it was said, were Mexican outlaws from Sonora and Chihuahua. Some were half-breed Indians, and a few were white gunmen who killed for the very joy of killing.

And The Terror himself? That was the mystery. Nobody knew his identity. Some rumors held that he was a white man; others maintained that he was a full-blooded Comanche Indian. Nobody had ever seen his face, for he always was masked. His deeds were enough. No torture was too cruel for his insane mind. No risk was too great, if he could obtain loot. With his band behind him, no man was safe on the Staked Plains. Many a smoldering pile of human bones testified to that.

As the Texan approached the outfit, he could hear the sharp crack of the bull whips and the hoarse shouts of the drivers. Twenty-two wagons, and in single file! Against the blue of the horizon, they made a pretty sight, with their white coverings. Kid Wolf, however, was not concerned with the beauty of the picture. Great danger threatened them, and it was his duty to be of what assistance he could. Touching his big white horse

14

with the spur, he came upon the long train's flank.

Ahead of the train were the scouts, or pathfinders. In the rear was the beef herd, on which the outfit depended for food. Behind that was the rear guard, armed with Winchesters.

The Texan neared the horseman at the head of the train, raising his arm in the peace signal. To his surprise, one of the scouts threw up his rifle! There was a puff of white smoke, and a bullet whistled over Kid Wolf's head.

"The fools!" muttered the Texan. "Can't they see I'm a friend?"

Setting his teeth, he rode ahead boldly, risking his life as he did so, for by this time several others had lifted their guns.

The six men who made up the advance party, eyed him sullenly as he drew up in front of them. The Texan found himself covered by half a dozen Winchesters.

"Who are yuh, and what do yuh want?" one of them demanded.

"I'm Kid Wolf, from Texas, sah. I have impo'tant news fo' the leader of this outfit."

One of the sextet separated himself from the others and came so close to the Texan that their horses almost touched.

"I'm in command!" he barked. "My name's Modoc. I'm in charge o' this train, and takin' it to Sante Fe."

The man, Modoc, was an impressive individual, bulky and stern. His face was thinner than the rest of his body, and Kid Wolf was rather puzzled to read the surly eyes that gleamed at him from under the bushy black brows. He was more startled still, however, when Modoc whispered in a voice just loud enough for him to hear:

"What color will the moon be tonight?"

Kid Wolf stared in astonishment. Was the man insane?

CHAPTER II

A THANKLESS TASK

Modoc waited, as if for an answer, and when it did not come, his face took on an expression of anger, in which cunning seemed to be mingled.

"What's yore message?" he rasped.

It took Kid Wolf several seconds to recover his composure. Was the wagon train being led to its doom by a madman? What did Modoc mean by his low-voiced, mysterious query? Or did he mean anything at all? The Texan put it down as the raving of a mind unbalanced by hardship and peril.

"I suppose yo'-all know," he drawled loudly enough for them all to hear, "that yo're on the most dangerous paht of the Llano, and that yo're off the road to Santa Fe."

"Yo're a liar!" the train commander snarled.

Kid Wolf tried to keep his anger from mounting. This was the thanks he got for trying to help these people!

16

"I'll prove it," sighed the kid patiently. "What rivah was that yo' crossed a few days ago?"

"Why, the Red River; we crossed it long ago," Modoc sneered. "Yo're either a liar or a fool, Kid! And I'd advise yuh to mind yore own business."

"Call me 'Wolf,'" said the Texan, a ring of steel in his voice. "I'm just 'The Kid' to friends. Others call me by mah last name. And speakin' of the trail, that wasn't the Red Rivah yo' crossed. It was the Wichita. And yo' must have gone ovah the Wichita Mountains, too."

"The Wichita!" ejaculated one of the other men. "Why, Modoc, yuh told us—"

"And I told yuh right!" said the leader furiously. "I've been over this route before, and I know just where we are."

"Yo're in The Terror's territory," drawled The Kid softly. "And I've heahd from a reliable source that he's planned to raid yo'."

The others paled at the mention of The Terror. But Modoc raised his voice in fury.

"Who are yuh goin' to believe?" he shouted. "This upstart, or me? Why, for all we know"—his voice dropped to a taunting sneer—"he might be a spy for The Terror himself—probably measurin' the strength of our outfit!"

The other men seemed to hesitate. Then one of them spoke out:

"Reckon we'll believe you, Modoc. We don't know this man, and we've trusted yuh so far."

Modoc grinned, showing a line of broken and

tobacco-stained teeth. He looked at Kid Wolf triumphantly.

"Now I'll tell you a few things, my fine young fellow," he leered. "Burn the wind out o' here and start pronto, before yuh get a bullet through yuh. Savvy?"

Kid Wolf decided to make one last appeal. If Modoc were insane, it seemed terrible that these others should be led to their doom on that account. Only the Texan could fully appreciate their peril. The wagon train was loaded with valuable goods, for these men were traders. The Terror would welcome such plunder, and it was his custom never to leave a man alive to carry the tale.

"Men," he said, "yo'-all got to believe me! Yo're in terrible danger, and off the right road. One man has already given his life to save yo', and now I'm ready to give mine, if necessary. Let me stay with yo' and guide yo' to safety, fo' yo' own sakes! Mah two guns are at yo' service, and if The Terror strikes, I'll help yo' fight."

The advance guard heard him out. Unbelief was written on all their faces.

"I think yuh'd better take Modoc's advice," one of them said finally, "and git! We can take care of ourselves."

His heart heavy, Kid Wolf shrugged and turned away. The rebuff hurt him, not on his own account, but because these blindly trusting men were being deceived. Modoc, whether purposely or not, had led them astray.

He was about to ride away when his eyes fell upon

the foremost of the wagons, which was now creaking up, pulled by its straining team. Kid Wolf gave a start. Thrust out of the opening in the canvas was a child's head, crowned with golden hair. There were women and children, then, in this ill-fated outfit!

The Texan rode his horse over to the wagon and smiled at the youngster. It was a boy of three, chubby-faced and brown-eyed.

"Hello, theah," Kid called. "What's yo' name?"

The baby returned the smile, obviously interested in this picturesque stranger.

"Name's Jimmy Lee," was the lisped answer. "I'm goin' to Santa Fe. Where you goin'?"

Kid Wolf gulped. He could not reply. There was small chance that this little boy would ever reach Santa Fe, or anywhere else. Tears came to his eyes, and he wheeled Blizzard fiercely.

"Good-by!" came the small voice.

"Good-by, Jimmy Lee," choked the Texan.

When he looked back again at the wagon train, he could still see a small, golden head gleaming in the first prairie schooner.

"Blizzahd," muttered Kid Wolf, "we've just got to help those people, whethah they want it or not."

He pretended to head eastward, but when he was out of sight of the wagon train, he circled back and drummed west at a furious clip. The only thing he could do, he saw now, was to go to Santa Fe for help. With the obstinate traders headed directly across the Llano, they were sure to meet with trouble. If he could bring back a company of soldiers from that Mexican settlement, he might aid them in time.

"If they won't let me help 'em at this end," he murmured, "I'll have to help 'em at the othah."

The town of Santa Fe—long rows of flat-topped adobes nestling under the mountain—was at that day under Spanish rule. Only a few Americans then lived within its limits.

It was a thriving, though sleepy, town, as it was the gateway to all Chihuahua. A well-beaten trail left it southward for El Paso, and its main street was lined with *cantinas*—saloons where mescal and tequila ran like water. There were gambling houses of ill repute, an open court for cockfighting, and other pastimes. The few gringos who were there looked, for the most part, like outlaws and fugitives from the States.

It lacked a few hours until sunset when Kid Wolf drummed into the town. The mountains were already beginning to cast long shadows, and the sounds of guitars and singing were heard in the gay streets.

Galloping past the plazas, the Texan at once went to the presidio—the palace of the governor. It was of adobe, like the rest of the buildings, but the thick walls were ornately decorated with stone. It was a fortress as well as a dwelling place, and it contained many rooms. Several dozen rather ragged soldiers were loafing about the presidio when Kid Wolf reached it, for a regiment was stationed in the town.

Kid Wolf sought an interview with the governor at

once, but in spite of his pleading, he was told to return in two hours. "The most honored and respected Governor Manuel Quiroz," it seemed, was busy. If the señor would return later, Governor Quiroz would be highly pleased to see him.

There was nothing to do but wait, and the Texan decided to be patient. He spent an hour in caring for his horse and eating his own hasty meal. Then, finding some time on his hands, he walked through the plaza, watching the crowds with eyes that missed nothing.

He found himself in a street where frijoles, peppers, and other foods were being offered for trade or barter. Cooking was even being done in open-air booths, and the air was heavy with seasoning and spice. Here and there was a drinking place, crowded with revelers. It was evidently some sort of feast day in Santa Fe.

In front of one of the wine shops a little knot of men and soldiers had gathered. All were flushed with drink and talking loudly in their own tongue. One of them— a captain in a gaudy uniform—saw the Texan and made a laughing remark to his companions.

Kid Wolf's face flushed under its tan. His eyes snapped, but he continued his walk. He had too much on his mind just then to resent insults.

But the captain had noticed his change of expression. The gringo, then, knew Spanish. His remarks became louder, more offensive. More than half intoxicated, he called jeeringly:

"I was just saying, señor, that many men who wear two guns do not know how to use even one. You understand, señor? Or perhaps the señor does not know the Spanish?"

Kid Wolf turned quietly.

"The señor knows the Spanish," he said softly.

The captain turned to his companions with a knowing wink. Then he addressed the Texan.

"Then, amigo, that is well," he mocked. "Perhaps the señor can shoot also. Perhaps the señor could do this."

A peon stood near by, and the captain pulled off the fellow's straw sombrero and tossed it into the street. The wind caught it and the hat sailed for some distance. With a quick movement the Spanish captain drew a pistol from his belt and fired. With a sharp report, a round, black hole appeared in the hat, low in the crown.

The crowd murmured its admiration at this feat. The captain stroked his thin black mustache and smiled proudly.

"Perhaps the señor might find that difficult to do," he mocked.

"Quién sabe?" Kid Wolf shrugged and started to pass on. He did not care to make a public exhibition of his shooting, especially when he had graver matters on his mind. But the jeers and taunts that broke loose from the half-drunken assembly were more than any man could endure, especially a Texan with fiery Southern blood in his veins. He turned, smiling. His eyes, however, were as cold as ice.

"Why," he asked calmly, "should I mutilate this po' man's hat?" His words were spoken in perfectly accented Spanish.

22

"The hat? Ah," mocked the captain, "if the señor hits it, I will pay for it with gold."

Kid Wolf drew his left-hand Colt so quickly that no man saw the motion. Before they knew it, there was a sudden report that rolled out like thunder—six shots, blended into one stuttering explosion. He had emptied his gun in a breath!

A gust of wind blew away the cloud of black powder smoke, and the crowd stared. Then some one began to laugh. It was taken up by others. Even the customers in the booths chuckled at Kid Wolf's discomfiture. The captain's laugh was the loudest of all.

"Six shots the señor took," he guffawed, "and missed with them all! Ah, didn't I tell you that the Americans are bluffers, like their game of poker? This one carries two guns and cannot use even one!"

Kid Wolf smiled quietly. A faint look of amusement was in his eyes.

"Maybe," he drawled, "yo'-all had bettah look at that hat."

Curiously, and still smiling, some of the loiterers went over to examine the target. When they had done so, they cried out in amazement. It was true that just one bullet hole showed in the front of the sombrero. The captain's shot had drilled that one. Naturally all had supposed that the gringo had missed. Such was not the case. All of Kid Wolf's six bullets had passed through the captain's bullet mark! For the back of the hat was torn by the marks of seven slugs! Some one held the sombrero aloft, and the excited crowd roared its approval and enthusiasm. Never had such shooting been seen within the old city of Santa Fe.

The Spanish captain, after his first gasp of surprise, had nothing to say. Chagrin and disgust were written over his face. If ever a man was crestfallen, the captain was. He hated to be made a fool of, and this quiet man from Texas had certainly accomplished it.

He was about to slink off when Kid Wolf drawled after him:

"Oh, captain! Pahdon, but haven't yo' forgotten somethin'?"

"What do you mean?" snapped the other.

"Yo' were goin' to pay for this man's sombrero, I believe," said Kid Wolf softly, "in gold."

"Bah!" snarled the officer. "That I refuse to do!"

The Texan's hand snapped down to his right Colt. A blaze of flame leaped from the region of his hip. Along with the crashing roar of the explosion came a sharp, metallic twang.

The bullet had neatly clipped away the captain's belt buckle! A yell of laughter rang out on all sides. For the captain's trousers, suddenly unsupported, slipped down nearly to his knees. With a cry of dismay, the disgruntled officer seized them frantically and held them up.

"Reach down in those," drawled the Texan, "and see if yo' can't find that piece of gold!"

The officer, white with rage in which hearty fear was mingled, obeyed with alacrity, pulling out a gold coin and handing it, with an oath, to the peon whose hat he had ruined.

"Muchas gracias," murmured Kid Wolf, reholstering his gun. "And now, if the fun's ovah, I must bid yo' *buenas tardes.* Adios!"

And doffing his big hat, the Texan took his departure with a sweeping bow, leaving the captain glaring furiously after him.

CHAPTER III

THE GOVERNOR'S ANSWER

J udging that it was almost time for his interview with the governor, Kid Wolf saddled Blizzard in the public *establo,* or stable, and rode at once to the governor's palace.

Although it did not occur to him that Quiroz would reject his plea for aid, he was filled with foreboding. He had a premonition that made him uneasy, although there seemed nothing at which to be alarmed.

Dismounting, he walked up the stone flags toward the presidio entrance—a huge, grated door guarded by two flashily dressed but barefooted soldiers. They nodded for him to pass, and the Texan found himself in a long, half-lighted passage. Another guard directed him into the office of Governor Quiroz, and Kid Wolf stepped through another carved door, hat in hand.

He found that he had entered a large, cool room, lighted softly by windows of brightly colored glass and barred with wrought iron. The tiles of the floor were in black-and-white design, and the place was bare of furniture, except at one end, where a large desk stood.

Behind it, in a chair of rich mahogany, sat an impressive figure. It was the governor.

While bowing politely, the Texan searched the pale face of the man of whom he had heard so much. By looking at him, he thought he discovered why Quiroz was so feared by the oppressed people of the district. Iron strength showed itself in the official's aristocratic features.

There was something there besides power. Quiroz had eyes that were mysterious and deep. Not even the Texan could read the secrets they masked. Cruelty might lurk there, perhaps, or friendliness—who could say? At the governor's soft-spoken invitation, Kid Wolf took a chair near the huge desk.

"Your business with me, señor?" asked the official in smoothly spoken English.

Kid Wolf spoke respectfully, although he did not fawn over the dignitary or lose his own quiet self-assertion. He was an American. He told of finding the tortured prospector and of the plight of the approaching wagon train.

"If they continue on the course they are followin'," guv'nor," he concluded, "they'll nevah reach Santa Fe. And I have every reason to believe that The Terror plans to raid them."

"And what," asked the governor pleasantly, "do you expect me to do?"

"I thought, sah," Kid Wolf replied, "that yo' would let me return to them with a company of yo' soldiers."

"My dear señor," the governor said with suave courtesy, "the people you wish to rescue are not subjects of mine."

Kid Wolf tried not to show the irritation he felt. "Surely, sah, yo' are humane enough to do this thing. I thought I told yo' theah's women and children in the wagon train."

Quiroz rubbed his chin as if in thought. His eyes, however, seemed to smolder with an emotion of which Kid Wolf could only guess the nature. The Spaniard's face was that of a hypnotist, with its thin, high-bridged nose and its chilling, penetrating gaze.

"Your name, señor?"

"Kid Wolf, from Texas, sah."

Spanish governors of that day had no reason to like gunmen from the Lone Star State. From the time of Santa Anna, Texas fighters had been thorns in their sides. But if Quiroz was thinking of this, he made no sign. He smiled with pleasure, either real or assumed.

"That is good," he said. "Señor Wolf, to show your good faith, will you be kind enough to lay your weapons on my desk? It is a custom here not to come armed in the presence of the governor."

Suspicion began to burn strongly in the back of the Texan's brain. Was Quiroz playing a crafty game? He was supposed to be friendly toward those from the States, but once before, in California, Kid Wolf had had dealings with a Spanish governor. Instantly he

27

was on his guard, although he did not allow his face to show it.

"I am an American, sah," he replied. "Some have called me a soldier of misfohtune. Anyway, I try and do good. What good I have done fo' the weak and oppressed, sah, I've done with these." The Kid tapped his twin Colts and went on: "I've twelve lead aces heah, sah, and I'm not in the habit of layin' 'em down."

"We're not playing cards, señor." Quiroz smiled pleasantly.

"No." Kid Wolf's quick smile flashed. "But if a game is stahted, I want a hand to play with."

His eyes were fixed on the carved front of the governor's desk. There seemed something strange about the carved design. He was seated directly in front of it, in the chair Quiroz had pointed out to him, and for the last few minutes he had wondered what it was that had attracted his attention.

The desk was carved with a series of squares chiseled deep into the dark wood. In one of the squares was a black circle about the size of a small silver piece. Somehow Kid Wolf did not like the looks of it. What it could be, he could hardly guess. The Texan had learned not to take chances. Slowly, and with his eyes still on the official's smiling face, he edged his chair away from it, an inch at a time. His progress was slow enough not to attract Quiroz's attention.

"Then," asked the governor slowly, "you refuse, señor?"

"Yo'-all are a fine guessah, sah!" snapped the Texan, alert as a steel spring.

The governor moved his knee. There was a sharp report, and a streak of flame leaped from the desk front, followed by a puff of blue smoke. The bullet, however, knocked a slab of plaster from the opposite wall. Just in time, Kid Wolf had moved his chair from the range of the trap gun.

Quiroz's death-dealing apparatus had failed. The Texan's cleverness had matched his own. Concealed in the desk had been a pistol, the trigger of which had been pressed by the weight of the official's knee on a secret panel. Quick as a flash, Kid Wolf was on his feet, hands flashing down toward his two .45s!

The governor, however, was not in the habit of playing a lone hand against any antagonist. Behind Kid Wolf rang out a command in curt Spanish:

"Hands up!"

Kid Wolf's sixth sense warned him that he was covered with a dead drop. His mind worked rapidly. He could have drawn and taken the governor of Santa Fe with him to death, perhaps cutting down some of the men behind him, as well. But in that case, what would become of the wagon train, with no one to save them from The Terror? A vision of the little golden-haired child crossed his mind. No, while there was life, there was hope. Slowly he took his hands away from his gun handles and raised them aloft.

Turning, he saw six soldiers, each with a rifle aimed at his breast. In all probability they had had their eyes on him during his audience with the governor. Quiroz snarled an order to them.

"Take away his guns!" he cried. Then, while the Texan was being disarmed, he took a long black cigarette from a drawer and lighted it with trembling fingers.

"You are clever, señor," said the governor, recovering his composure. "I am exceedingly sorry, but I will have to deal with you in a way you will not like—the adobe wall." Quiroz bowed. "I bid you adios." He turned to his soldiers. "Take him to the *calabozo!*" he ordered sharply.

The building that was then being used as Santa Fe's prison was constructed of adobe with tremendously thick walls and no windows. The only place light and air could enter the sinister building was through a grating the size of a man's hand in the huge, rusty iron door.

Kid Wolf was marched to the prison by his sextet of guards. While the door was being opened, he glanced around him, taking what might prove to be his last look at the sky. His eyes fell upon one of the walls of the jail. It was pitted with hundreds of little holes. The Texan smiled grimly. He knew what had made them—bullets. It was the execution place!

The door clanged behind him, and a scene met The Kid's eyes that caused him to shudder. In the big, dank room were huddled fourteen prisoners. Most of them were miserable, half-naked peons. It was intolerably

30

hot, and the air was so bad as almost to be unbreathable.

The prisoners kept up a wailing chant—a hopeless prayer for mercy and deliverance. A guttering candle shed a ghastly light over their thin bodies.

So this was what his audience with the governor had come to! What a tyrant Quiroz had proved to be! Strangely enough, The Kid's thoughts were not of his own terrible plight, but of the peril that awaited the wagon train. If he could only escape this place, he might at least help them. What a mistake he had made in going to the governor for aid!

His next thought was of his horse, Blizzard. What would become of him, if he, Kid Wolf, died? The Texan knew one thing for certain, that Blizzard was free. Nobody could touch him save his master. He was also sure that the faithful animal awaited his beck and call. The white horse was somewhere near and on the alert. Kid Wolf had trained it well.

He soon saw that escape by ordinary means from the prison was quite hopeless. There was no guard to over-power, the walls were exceedingly thick, and the door impregnable.

Only one of the prisoners, Kid Wolf noted, was an American—a sickly faced youth of about the Texan's own age. A few questions brought out the information that all the inmates of the jail were under sentence of death.

The hours passed slowly in silent procession while the dying candle burned low in the poison-laden air. Kid Wolf paced the floor, his eyes cool and serene.

His mind, however, was wide awake. When was he to be shot? In the morning? Or would his execution be delayed, perhaps for days?

The Texan never gave up hope, and he was doing more than hoping now—he was planning carefully. Kid Wolf had a hole card. Had the Spanish soldiers known him better, they would have used more care in disarming him. But then, enemies of Kid Wolf had made that mistake before, to their sorrow.

Clearly enough, he could not help the wagon train where he was. He must get out. But the only way to get out, it seemed, was to go out with the firing squad—a rather unpleasant thing to do, to say the least.

The tiny grated square in the jail door began to lighten. It grew brighter. Day was breaking.

"It will soon be time for the beans," muttered the American youth.

"Will they give us breakfast?" asked the Texan.

The other laughed bitterly. "We'll have beans," he said shortly, "but we won't eat them."

Not long afterward the iron door opened, and two soldiers entered, carrying a red earthenware olla. "Fifteen men," said one of them in Spanish, "counting the new one."

"Fifteen men," chanted the other in singsong voice. "Fifteen beans."

Kid Wolf's brows began to knit. At first he had thought that the beans meant breakfast. Now he saw that something sinister was intended. Some sort of lottery was about to be played with beans.

"There are fourteen white beans," the young American whispered, "and one black one. We all draw. The man who gets the black bean dies this morning."

The hair prickled on the Texan's head. Every morning these unfortunates were compelled to play a grim game with death.

The prisoners were all quaking with terror, as they came up to the ugly red jug to take their chance for life. As much as these miserable men suffered in this terrible place, existence was still dear to them.

One soldier shook the beans in the olla; the other stood back against the wall with leveled gun to prevent any outbreak. Then the lottery began.

Kid Wolf viewed the situation calmly, and decided that to try to wrest the weapon from the soldier would be folly. Other soldiers were watching through the grated door.

One by one, the prisoners drew. The opening in the olla was just large enough for a hand to be admitted. All was blind chance, and no one could see what he had drawn until his bean was out of the jug. Some of the peons screamed with joy after drawing their white beans. The black one was still in the jar.

The two white men were the last to draw. Both took their beans and stepped to one side to look at them. It was an even break. Kid Wolf was smiling; the other was trembling.

The eyes of Kid Wolf met the fear-stricken eyes of the other. They stood close together. Each had looked at his bean. The sick man's face had gone even whiter.

"I'll trade yo' beans," offered the Texan.

"Mine's—black!" gasped the other.

"I know," The Kid whispered in reply. "Trade with me!"

"It means that yuh give yore life for mine," was the agonized answer. "I can't let yuh do that."

"Believe me or not, but I have a plan," urged the Texan in a low tone. "And it might work. Hurry."

The color returned to the sick youth's face as the beans were cautiously exchanged. Then Kid Wolf turned to the soldiers and displayed a black bean.

"Guess I'm the unlucky one." He smiled whimsically. He turned to the sick boy for a final handshake. "Good luck," he whispered, "and if my plans fail, adios forever."

"Come!" ordered a Spanish soldier.

Waving his hand in farewell, Kid Wolf stepped out to meet the doom that had been prepared for him.

CHAPTER IV

SURPRISES

At the prison door, Kid Wolf was met by a squad of ten soldiers. It was the firing squad. The Texan fell in step with them and was marched around the building to the bullet-scarred wall. Kid Wolf faced the rising sun. Was he now seeing it for the last time?

If he was afraid, he made no sign. His expression was

unruffled and calm. He was smiling a little, and his arms, as he folded them on his breast, did not tremble in the slightest.

The officer who was to have charge of the execution had not yet appeared on the scene, and the soldiers waited with their rifle stocks trailing in the sand.

Then there was a quick bustle. The officer sauntered around the corner of the building, his bright uniform making a gay sight in the early sun. He was a captain—the captain whom Kid Wolf had humiliated the afternoon before! The eyes of the Spanish officer, when they fell upon his victim, widened with surprise which at once gave way to exultation.

"Ah, it is my amigo—the señor of the two guns!" he cried.

It was his day of revenge! The captain could not conceal his joy at this chance to square things with his enemy for good and all. He did not try to. His laugh was sneering and amused.

"And to think it will be me—Captain Hermosillo—who will say the word to fire!" He turned to his soldiers in high good humor and waved his sword. "At twenty paces," he ordered. "We shall soon see how bravely the señor dies. Ready!"

The rifle mechanisms clattered sharply.

Then the captain turned to his victim, an insolent smile on his cruel features. "Will the señor have his eyes bandaged? Blindfolded, yes?"

Kid Wolf returned the smile. "Yes," he replied quietly. "Maybe yo' better blindfold me."

Hermosillo laughed tauntingly and turned to wink at his men. "He is brave, yes!" he mocked. "He cannot endure seeing the *carabinas* aimed at his heart. He wants his eyes bandaged—the *muchos grande Americano!* Ah, the coward!" He spat contemptuously on the sand. "He does not know how to face the guns. Well, we will humor him!"

The captain whipped a silk handkerchief from his pocket and stepped forward. Kid Wolf's eyes were gleaming with icy-blue lights. This was the moment he had been waiting for! That handkerchief was a necessary cog in his carefully laid plans. Captain Hermosillo was soon to learn just how cowardly this young Texan was. And the surprise was not going to be pleasant.

Kid Wolf's hole card was a big bowie knife—the same weapon that had played such havoc at the Alamo. He carried it in a strange hiding place—tucked into a leather sheath sewn to the inside of his shirt collar, between his shoulder blades. That knife had rescued Kid Wolf from many a tight situation, and he had practiced until he could draw it with all the speed of heat lightning.

When the captain placed the handkerchief over his eyes, Kid Wolf reached back, as if pretending to assist him. Like a flash, his fingers closed over the bone handle of the knife instead. Hermosillo found himself with the cold point of the gleaming bowie pressed against his throat!

At the same time, Kid Wolf whirled his body about so

that the officer was between him and the firing squad. His left hand held the captain in a grip of steel; his right held the glittering blade against Hermosillo's Adam's apple!

"Throw down yo' rifles and back away from 'em!" Kid Wolfe called to the soldiers. "Pronto! Or I'll kill yo' captain!"

Hermosillo gave an agonized yell of fear. In a voice of quaking terror, he ordered his men to do what Kid Wolf had commanded them. His breath was coming in wheezing gasps.

The firing squad, taken aback by this sudden development—for only a few seconds had passed since The Kid had drawn the knife—hesitated, and then obeyed. At best, they were none too quick-thinking, and they saw that their leader was in a perilous plight. Their *carabinas* thudded to the sand.

"Buena!" laughed the Texan boyishly.

He pushed the captain just far enough away for him to be in good hitting range. Then he lashed out at him with his hard fist, catching the fear-crazed officer directly on the point of the jaw. Many pounds of lean muscle were behind the blow, and Hermosillo landed ten feet away in a cloud of dust.

The Texan lost no time in whirling on his feet and sprinting for the corner of the building. He reached it just in time to bump into another officer, who was just then arriving on the scene. Kid Wolf snatched the pistol from his belt and sent him up against the wall with a jar. Before the disarmed Spaniard knew what had happened, he was sitting on the ground, nursing a bruised jaw, and Kid Wolf was gone!

The Texan found the streets deserted at that early hour. Racing across the plaza, he raised his voice in a coyote yell:

"Yip, yip, yipee-e-e!"

It was answered by an eager whinny. It was Blizzard! The horse, waiting patiently in the vicinity, knew that signal. It came running down another street like a white snowstorm.

Kid Wolf ran to meet the horse. A sharp rattle of rifle fire rang out behind him. The soldiers had given chase! A bullet zipped the stone flags under his feet; another smacked solidly into the corner of an adobe house.

The alarm had been given. Two gayly uniformed officers ran into the street from the direction of the presidio. They were trying to head the Texan off, attempting to get between him and his horse.

But Blizzard was coming at too hot a pace. The two Spaniards cut in just as Kid Wolf leaped to the saddle. He fired the pistol's single barrel at one of the officers, and hurled the useless weapon into the other's face.

"Come on, Blizzahd!" Kid Wolf sang out. "Let's go from heah!"

The powerful animal's hoofs thundered against the flagstones, leaped a stone wall, and charged down the street. Behind them, already organized, came the pursuit. To Kid Wolf's ears came the whine of bullets.

"From now on," he cried to his plunging horse, "it

all depends on yo'-all! Burn that wind!"

Once Blizzard had hit his stride, Kid Wolf knew that no horse in Santa Fe could catch him. Striking off to the eastward in the direction of the Staked Plains, the Texan gave his animal free rein.

The pursuit was dropping behind, a few yards at a time. Instead of buzzing around his ears now, the bullets were falling short, kicking up spurts of dust. The cries in angry Spanish grew fainter until they died into a confused hubbub. Kid Wolf had left the town behind him and was racing out over the level plain. Looking back, he could see a score or more of brown clouds—dirt stirred by the horsemen who were now almost lost from view. These dwindled. In an hour only half a dozen riders remained on his trail. Blizzard was still going strong.

Out on the great Llano Estacado, The Kid managed, by superior horsemanship, to give the balance of his pursuers the slip. When he had succeeded in confusing them, he slowed his faithful mount down for a needed rest. And now where was the wagon train? Where was he to find it? A chill raced down his spine. Had The Terror already struck? The thought of the women and children in the hapless outfit filled him with a feeling akin to panic. He must find the wagon train. It might not yet be too late.

Kid Wolf was a plainsman. He could locate water where none appeared to exist; he could discover game when older men failed; and he could follow a course on the limitless prairie as surely as a sailor could navigate the seas by means of his compass. By day or by night, he was "trailwise."

Carefully Kid Wolf estimated the route the wagon train had been taking. Then he figured out the progress it had probably made since he had left it. In this way he fixed a point in his mind—an imaginary dot that he must reach if he meant to find the prairie schooners. If Modoc—the leader of the outfit—had kept to his original course, The Kid could not fail to meet them.

Accordingly, Kid Wolf traveled all the rest of that day in a straight line, marking his course by the sun. He stopped only once at noon for water and a short rest, going on again until dusk.

At nightfall, he made camp and lay awake, looking at the stars overhead. His thoughts were of The Terror and of his intended victims. Strangely enough, the face of Modoc came into his reflections, also. He could not dismiss him. Was he really insane, or was it just obstinacy? If the latter, what had he meant by his strange expression: "What color will the moon be tonight?" Kid Wolf thought for a long time and then gave it up.

He did not fear any further pursuit by the Spanish soldiers. The trail he had left behind was too puzzling; he had taken care of that. Besides, he knew that the average Spaniard feared the Apache and the other Indian tribes that infested portions of the Staked Plains. If there were any danger during the night, Blizzard would give him warning.

He was up with the dawn. At its first faint, pinkish glow, he was in the saddle again. The day promised to be hot. The midsummer sun had burned the grass to a crisp brown. By midday, mirages began to show in hollows. Heat flickered. Both horse and rider drank at a pool of yellow-brown water and pressed on.

Late in the afternoon, Kid Wolf made out a faint white line on the far horizon. It was the wagon train! He sighed with relief. The Terror, then, had not yet raided it. For The Terror left only destruction in his wake. Had he already plundered it, he would have burned the wagons to the ground.

Increasing his speed, Kid Wolf rapidly approached it. As he came nearer, he saw that the outfit was in the center of a field of alkali and making slow and painful progress. He did not see the beef herd. Plainly, something had happened during his absence.

Kid Wolf rode in, waving his hat. Would he get a bullet for his pains? He kept his eyes open as he drummed in over the alkali flat.

Modoc and three others were at the head of the outfit. They recognized him at once. Modoc started to raise his rifle. One of the others struck the weapon down. Obviously the train commander had lost some of his influence. Another of the pathfinders shouted for Kid Wolf to come on. A dozen of the travelers left their wagons and came forward. This time they seemed glad to see Kid Wolf.

"Yuh was right, after all!" one of them cried. "Modoc led us out of the way. We're lost!"

"I meant all right," Modoc grumbled. "I did my best—must have made a mistake somewhere. I'll find the trail, never worry. And if yuh take my advice, yuh'll drive this four-flusher away from here! He don't mean us any good, What business is it of his?"

Kid Wolf sternly pointed back to the wagons.

"Those women and children theah," he snapped, "is mah business."

"Shut up, Modoc!" ordered one of the men. "We trust this man, and we believe he's our friend." He turned to the Texan. "Yuh can consider yoreself in command here now," he added.

Modoc trembled with ungovernable anger, but, out-numbered as he was, he could say nothing. Sulkily he returned to his own wagon.

From the drivers, Kid Wolf learned a story of hard-ship and semi-starvation. Indians had driven away their beef herd, leaving them without food. All day they had had nothing to eat, and were at the point of killing and devouring prairie dogs. The water, too, was bad—so full of alkali as nearly to be undrinkable, and as bitter as gall.

Kid Wolf lost no time in taking the situation in hand. His own provisions he turned over to the women and children of the outfit. Then he changed the course of the train so that it led toward civilization. At nightfall they made camp by a pool of fair drinking water. The outfit told him that as yet they had seen no sign of The Terror.

"Probably we won't," said one.

Kid Wolf was not so optimistic. That night he bor-rowed two .45 Colt revolvers from the wagon-train sup-

42

plies. He selected them with extreme care, testing them by shooting at marks. So accurate was his shooting that the men of the outfit could not conceal their admiration. The first weapon he tried threw the shots an inch or two to one side, but he finally obtained a pair that worked perfectly. Then he sanded the wooden handles of the guns to roughen them slightly.

"It nevah pays to have yo' hand slip when makin' a draw," he explained.

The outfit's camp fire was shielded with canvas that night, at Kid's suggestion. On that wide plain a light showed for many miles, and it was poor policy to advertise one's position.

Tired as he was, Kid Wolf rose at midnight, after sleeping a few hours. He wanted to be sure that everything was well. Making a tour of the wagon train, he suddenly stopped in his tracks and sniffed. There was no mistaking the delicious odor. It made Kid Wolf hungry. It was frying meat. The Texan quietly aroused some of the men and led them to one of the wagons.

"I want yo'-all to see fo' yo'selves," he explained.

The wagon was Modoc's own, and they entered it. The ex-wagon train commander had a shielded lantern burning inside, and he was in the act of eating a big supper! When he saw that he had visitors, he tried to reach the gun belt he had hung up at one end of the wagon. Kid Wolf was too quick for him.

"Yo' call yo'self a man!" he murmured in a voice filled with contempt. "Why, a low-down coyote is a gentleman alongside of yo'. I wondered why yo' looked so well fed, while the rest of the camp was starvin'. Men, search this wagon!"

While Modoc swore, the search was made. It disclosed many pounds of dried beef and other provisions. It was Modoc's little private supply.

"We'll divide it up with everybody in the mohnin'," suggested the Texan, "with a double allowance fo' the children and the women."

The wagon men were so furious at Modoc's selfishness that they could have torn him to pieces. Kid Wolf, however, prevented the trouble that was brewing.

"Every one to their blankets, men," he said. "We can't affohd to fight among ouahselves just now."

When the camp was asleep again, he took up his lonely vigil. The night was pitch black, without moon or stars. A wind whispered softly across the great Llano.

Suddenly The Kid's attention was attracted by something on the western horizon. It seemed to be in the sky—a faint red glow, across which shadows appeared to move like phantoms. Like a picture from the ghost world, it flickered for a few minutes like heat lightning, then disappeared, leaving the night as dark as before. It was a night mirage, and something more than an optical illusion. It was a rare thing on the plain. The Kid knew that it meant something. That glow was the reflection in the sky of a camp fire! Those shadows were men! The Texan quickly told his sentinels.

"I'm ridin' out to see what it is," he said. "Keep a close watch while I'm gone. I'm on a little scoutin' pahty of mah own. It might be that Quiroz has followed me—which I doubt. And it might be—The Terror!"

Mounting Blizzard, he was quickly swallowed up in the darkness.

CHAPTER V

THE CAMP OF THE TERROR

K id Wolf knew that the camp fire was many miles away. He gave his horse just a touch of the spur—that was always enough for Blizzard—and they proceeded to split the wind. The horse was as sure-footed as a cat, and was not an animal to step into a prairie-dog hole, even on a black night. Blizzard had ample rest and water, and was never fresher. He ran like a greyhound.

Kid Wolf never forgot that gallop across the Llano by night. It was like running full tilt against an ever-opening velvet curtain. He could hardly see his horse's head.

Blizzard's hoofs pounded on and on across the level plateau. Miles disappeared under his flying feet, while Kid's keen eyes were fastened on the horizon ahead. Finally he made out an orange glow—a light that changed to a redder and redder hue until it became a point of fire. The Texan approached it rapidly, more and more cautious.

That was no small camp! Many men were around that flickering fire. Kid Wolf dismounted, whispering for

Blizzard to remain where he was. Then, like a slinking Apache Indian, he approached on foot, making no sound. Not once did his high-heeled boots snap a weed or rustle the dried grass. He would not have been more silent had he been wearing moccasins.

There were a hundred or more men in the camp. It was a small city. Kid Wolf could hear the champing and stamping of countless restless horses, and the men were thick around the fire. A conference of some kind was being held.

The Texan approached closer and closer, all eyes and ears. If he could discover the identity of this band and something of their plans—

Suddenly a sentry rose up from the grass not a yard from him. His eyes fell upon the intruder, and his mouth flew open. In his hand was a short-barreled carbine.

The Texan seized him, dodged under the half-raised weapon and cut off the man's cry with the pressure of a muscular hand. He fought noiselessly, and the sentry— a Mexican—was no match for him. Throwing him to the ground, Kid Wolf gagged him with the man's own gayly colored scarf. Then he bound him securely, using the sentry's sash and carbine strap.

Kid Wolf exchanged his hat for the Mexican's steep-crowned sombrero and picked up the carbine. In this guise he could approach the camp with comparative safety. Pulling the sombrero over his eyes, he came in closer to the camp fire. As he did so, a trio of men— two white men and one half-breed—came into the camp from another direction. The Kid heard one of the

46

other sentries hail the newcomers.

"What color will the moon be tonight?" was the challenge.

Thrills raced up Kid Wolf's spine. That was the question Modoc had asked him! What deep plot was behind that seemingly meaningless query? Then the Texan heard the response.

"The moon will be red!" was the countersign, and the trio passed and approached the ring around the fire.

There was no doubt now that he was in the camp of The Terror! The men outlined in the ruddy firelight were desperadoes. Never had the Texan seen such a gathering. Some were American gunmen, evil-faced and heavily armed. Others were Mexicans and Indians. There was a tenseness in the very atmosphere. As Kid Wolf came closer to the fire, he was hailed in turn:

"What color will the moon be tonight?"

"The moon will be red," Kid Wolf replied softly.

No one paid him any attention. All eyes were on a figure near the glowing fire.

The man was talking and seemed to be in authority. He was dressed in a red Mexican coat, rich silver-trimmed pantaloons, and carried a brace of gold-mounted pistols. His face was covered with a mask of black velvet. Instinctively Kid Wolf knew that he was looking at the dread scourge of the Llano Estacado—The Terror of the Staked Plains! The bandit, then, kept himself masked even in front of his own men! Kid Wolf, as he listened, grew tense. His eyes were shining with snapping blue fire. The Terror was planning a raid upon the wagon train! His voice, cold and deadly, came to Kid Wolf's ears:

"Everything, then, caballeros, is arranged. We strike at dawn and wipe them out, sparing nobody. If a man escapes, you are all running a risk, for some of you might be identified. Man, woman, and child, they must die! Our man, of course, you all know. Do not fire on him."

Kid Wolf listened to that sinister voice and wondered what the face behind the mask looked like. The bandit leader had no more soul than a rattler, and one might expect more mercy from a wolf. And Kid Wolf already knew whom The Terror meant when he spoke of "our man." Anger shook the Texan from head to foot. He had learned enough. The bandits were already about to mount their horses in order that they might reach the wagon train at daybreak. There was no time to lose. He must get back to the helpless outfit ahead of them.

Sauntering carelessly, he slipped out of the circle about the fire and made his way out of the camp without being noticed. Once out of the range of the firelight, he raced into the darkness for his horse.

Blizzard was waiting patiently. He had not moved from his tracks. An ordinary animal might have nickered upon scenting other horses, but Blizzard had been trained otherwise. Kid Wolf leaped into the saddle, slapped his mount gently on the neck, and was swallowed up in the night as Blizzard answered the summons.

● ● ●

The east was a pale line against the dark of the prairie night when Blizzard drummed up to the sleeping wagon train with his rider. It still lacked a half hour until the dawn.

The Texan sent the sentries to arouse every available fighting man in the wagon train.

"Is it The Terror?" one of them questioned, paling.

"It is," replied Kid Wolf. "We must act quickly."

In a few minutes men were pouring out of the wagons, weapons in their hands. It was just light enough now to see. Modoc ran out of his wagon, strapping on his Colt .45 as he came. He advanced toward the Texan sneeringly. The others gathered about to see what would happen. Something in Kid Wolf's eyes warned them of impending trouble.

"What's the idea now?" Modoc snarled, showing his stained teeth like a wolf. "Has this four-flusher been up to his tricks again?"

Kid Wolf's voice came cool and calm. "Modoc," he drawled, "what color will the moon be tonight?"

Modoc's face went the color of putty. Like a flash, the insolence had gone out of his eyes, to be replaced with fear. He moistened his lips feverishly.

"I—I don't know what yo're talkin' about," he stammered.

"Are yo' sure," said Kid Wolf with deadly quietness, "that the moon won't be red?"

Modoc began to tremble like a leaf. His gun hand moved part way to his hip, then stopped. Beads of per-

49

spiration stood out on his clammy forehead.

"Afraid to draw like a man?" the Texan drawled. "I wouldn't doubt it. Men, this man is a betrayah. He is one of The Terror's bandits. That's why he led yo' off the track. He brought yo' here to die like rats."

Modoc's face was blue-white as Kid Wolf continued:

"When I first showed up, Modoc thought I might be one of The Terror's messengahs. I didn't come through with the password, and he learned different. I didn't know what he meant, then, but I know now!"

The wagon men surged around Modoc threateningly. Fury was written over the faces of them all. There were cries of "Kill him!" "Hang the traitor!"

Kid Wolf still faced the fear-frozen Modoc, smiling coolly. There was quiet menace in that easy smile.

"I usually shoot the head off a rattlesnake when I see one," he said softly. "One day, yeahs ago, a rattlah killed a favorite dawg of mine. I blew that snake apart, bit by bit. Modoc, that snake was a gentleman alongside of yo'. I'm givin' yo' an even chance to kill me. Fill yo' hand!"

Modoc, with a wheezing, gasping breath, decided upon action. His hand streaked for his hip. But Kid Wolf had drawn a split second later and more than a split second faster. The fingers of his right hand closed upon the handle of one of his twin Colts. In the same instant, fire flew!

With the first explosion, Modoc grunted with pain, dropping his gun. The bullet had caught him squarely in the wrist, rendering his fingers useless. But Kid Wolf kept firing, although he did not aim for Modoc's head or body. His gun flashed and stuttered twice, three times, four—five—six! Dust flew from Modoc's coat sleeve as the bullets landed with a series of terrific smashes. As he had torn the rattlesnake bit by bit, Kid Wolf ripped Modoc's gun arm.

Each bullet took effect, and Modoc staggered from the impacts, knees slumping to the ground. The traitor would never use that gun arm again. It dangled from his body, broken and useless. The others would have literally torn Modoc limb from limb had not the Texan ordered otherwise.

"He doesn't deserve hangin'," he said, "so let him be. We've got work to do. The Terror and his gang will be here at any minute. Now listen carefully to what I say."

Quietly he gave his orders, and just as carefully, the wagon men carried them out. Under Kid Wolf's masterly leadership they had regained their nerve. Panic left them, and they became grim and determined.

The Kid learned that there were thirty-four men in the outfit. Thirty-four against at least a hundred! The odds were great, but the Texan had faced greater ones alone. With the train in the hands of Modoc—one of their own men—the marauders expected to take the outfit by surprise. Thanks to the Texan, all that was changed now. He gave orders that the wagons be shifted into a circle, with the children and women on the inside behind shelter. The men were posted in the wagons and behind them, Kid Wolf giving each man his station.

"Do not fiah until I give the coyote yell," he said. "And then keep yo' sights down. Shoot low!"

Kid Wolf himself took a position between two of the covered wagons, his horse Blizzard within quick call. In the narrow chink, just wide enough for him to ride his horse through, he placed three loaded Sharps .50-caliber rifles, ready for quick use.

They had not long to wait. Only a few minutes had elapsed after the wagons had been shifted when Kid Wolf saw a body of horsemen approaching from the west. It was The Terror's band! Dust stirred by the hoofs of a hundred galloping horses rose in the air like brown thunderclouds.

As the grim defenders watched, the band split up, divided into two rapidly moving lines, and began to surround the train in a sweeping circle. The circle formed, began to close in. Kid Wolf peered along the barrel of one of the Sharps rifles. Then, after what seemed minutes, he uttered his coyote cry:

"Yip, yip, yip-ee!"

It was followed by a terrific burst of fire from the wagon train. The signal had been given at the opportune time. The bandits faltered. They hadn't expected this! The Terror had hoped to find the wagon train still asleep and defenseless. The rolling powder smoke cleared away somewhat, and it could be seen that a dozen or more of the attackers had melted out of their saddles, like butter on a hot stove.

But the raiders, outnumbering the defenders and real-
izing it, still came on. Kid Wolf threw aside the rifle and
drew his twin .45s. Deliberately stepping out into the
open, he fanned the hammers from the level of his hip.
His waistline, as he swung the thundering Colts from
side to side, seemed to be alive with sputtering red
sparks. Smoke rolled around him. The bandits in front
of him dropped by twos and threes.

Holes appeared in this side of the bandits' circle—
holes that did not close up. Riderless mounts dashed
about frantically, their reins trailing; wounded horses
added to the uproar with their death screams. It was a
battle!

Seeing that the force of the charge had been broken
on this flank, Kid Wolf ran across to re-enforce the
other sides of the circle. At one point the outlaws had
already broken through the circle of wagons. Kid Wolf
sent three screaming slugs toward them, and they fell
back in disorder, leaving one desperado stretched out
behind them.

Reloading his guns, Kid Wolf climbed upon one of
the wagons and again opened fire; this time with such
an effect that all sides of the attacking circle began to
break and fall back to safety. Mere force of numbers
does not always count in a gun fight. Not more than half
a dozen of the defenders had been hit. The survivors
raised a hearty cheer. Kid Wolf's generalship had
beaten back the first outlaw charge!

It was then that Modoc played his final card. Hoping
to gain the protection of the outlaws, and fearing the

wagon train's vengeance, he slipped out of the circle of covered wagons and, on foot, began running. His goal was ahead of him, but he never reached it. His late comrades—the bandits—evidently thought he had played the traitor with them, for they fired on him relentlessly. He fell, then rose again to scramble on. Bullets kicked up the sod around him. Others plumped into his body. Again he fell, this time to stay. His body was riddled with scores of bullets. So died the traitor.

Kid Wolf knew that a certain advantage always lies with the offensive. Defenders haven't the power of attackers. The Texan decided to risk a countercharge. He knew that it might break down the courage of the bandit band. At least it would be a surprise. He called for volunteers.

"I want a dozen men who can shoot straight from the back of a runnin' hoss," he said. "It'll be dangerous. Who's with me?"

Immediately more men than he wanted spoke up. Quickly choosing twelve, he gave them their orders.

"At the next chahge," the Texan drawled, "we'll ride out theah and give 'em somethin' to think about. If I'm right, I think they'll scattah. If I'm wrong—well, they'll probably wipe us out. Are yo' game?"

The men were game, as the Texan soon found out. They were fighting for their families, as well as their own lives and possessions.

Again the attacking line of horsemen formed, and in a cloud of dust, they came at the wagon train. Their bullets cut slashes in the covered-wagon tops, smashed into wheels and wagon trees, and kicked up geysers of sand. They would be hard to stop this time!

But Kid Wolf gave the word for his own charge. He had several reasons for doing this. It amounted to folly in the eyes of some, but the Texan knew the value of a countercharge. And if he could bring down The Terror himself, he knew the battle was as good as won. Out of the wagon circle they came, saddle leather creaking and guns blazing! The Kid, on his snow-white charger, was in the lead. A lane opened in the bandit ranks as if by magic.

Kid Wolf pressed his quick advantage. His movement had taken the outlaw band by surprise. The utter recklessness of it shook their nerve.

Two of the wagon men fell. The others kept on, clearing a swathe with their sputtering Colts.

The bandits hesitated. The defenders who had remained behind the wagons kept up their deadly barrage. They were dropping accurately placed shots where they would be sure to do the most good. Then The Terror's band retreated, broke formation. The retreat became a rout—a mad getaway with every man for himself. Outnumbered as they were, the defenders were making more than a good account of themselves.

Kid Wolf's eyes sought for The Terror himself—and found him. His red coat and gay trappings were easy to locate, even in that mad stampede. The bandit chief was attempting to make his getaway. The Texan, however, cut him off after a hard, furious ride.

Separated from his men, The Terror turned in his

saddle, wildly attempting to get the drop on Kid Wolf as he came in. One of his gold-mounted pistols flashed. The bullet hissed over the Texan's head. He had dropped low in the saddle.

The Terror whirled his horse at Kid Wolf's. He realized that it was a fight to the end. He fired his other weapon almost in the Texan's face. The Kid, however, had pulled the trigger of his own gun just a fraction of a second before. The Terror's aim was spoiled just enough so that the bullet whined wide. The bandit chief collapsed in his saddle. He had been hit in the shoulder.

The Texan closed in. There was a violent shock as Blizzard thudded into the bandit's horse. The Terror, eyes glittering wickedly through the openings in his velvet mask, slid from his horse, landing feet first. With a glittering knife in his unwounded hand, he made a spring toward Kid Wolf. The blade would have buried itself in the Texan's thigh had not The Kid whirled his horse just in time.

"All right," said the Texan coolly. "We have it out with ouah hands."

Holstering his guns, he leaped from his horse. He scorned even to use his bowie knife, as he advanced toward the bandit at a half crouch. The Terror thought he had the advantage. The Kid's hands were bare of any weapons. With a snarl, the bandit chief leaped forward, knife swishing aloft. Never had Kid Wolf struck so hard a blow as he struck then! Added to the power of his own tremendous strength and leverage was The Terror's

56

own speed as he lunged in. Fist met jaw with a sickening thud.

The Terror was a big and heavy man. His weight was added to Kid Wolf's as both men came together. There was a snap as his head went back—went back at too great an angle. His neck was broken instantly. Without a moan, the bandit chief dropped limply to the sand, dead before he ever reached it!

Kid Wolf took a deep breath. Then he bent over the fallen man and jerked the velvet mask from his features. He gasped in amazement. It was Quiroz! For a moment the Texan could not believe his eyes. Then the truth began to dawn on him. The Terror and the tyrannical governor of Santa Fe were one and the same! Quiroz had led a double life for years, and had covered his tracks well. So powerful had he become that he had received the appointment as governor. No wonder he had refused Kid Wolf aid! And no wonder he had sought his life!

"Well, I guess his account is paid," said Kid Wolf grimly. "The Terror of the Staked Plains is no more."

He looked about him. The remainder of the bandits had made a thorough retreat, leaving a large number of their companions on the plain behind them. Their defeat had been complete and decisive.

"Bueno," said Kid Wolf.

"Oh, the cows stampede on the Rio Grande!
   The Rio!
The sand do blow, and the winds do wail,

But I want to be wheah the cactus stands!
  The Rio!
  And the rattlesnake shakes his ornery tail!"

The buckskin-clad singer raised his hat in happy farewell. The people of the wagon train answered his shout:

"Shore yo' won't go on with us?"

"We shore thank yuh for what yuh done, Kid!"

Others took up the cry. They hated to lose this smiling young Texan's company. He had saved them from death—and worse. Not only that, but they had learned to like him and depend on him.

The Texan, however, declined to stay longer. Nor would he listen to any thanks.

"Adios," he called, "and good luck! Wheahevah the weakah side needs a champion, theah yo'll find Kid Wolf. Somehow I always find lots to do. Heah's hopin' yo' won't evah need mah services again."

He caught sight of a golden-haired child beaming at him from one of the wagons.

"Good-by, Jimmy Lee!" he called.

He whirled in his saddle, touched Blizzard with the reins, and rode away at a long lope.

CHAPTER VI

ON THE CHISHOLM TRAIL

From the sweeps of high country bordering close upon Santa Fe, it was no easy journey to the Chisholm Trail, even for a trail-eating horse of Blizzard's caliber. But The Kid had taken his time. His ultimate destination, unless fate altered his plans, was his own homeland—the sandy Rio Grande country.

More than anything else, it was the thirst for adventure that led the buckskin-clad rider to the beaten cattle road which cut through wilderness and prairie from Austin to the western Kansas beef markets.

And now, after following the trail for one uneventful day, Kid Wolf had left it—in search of water. A line of lofty cottonwoods on the eastern horizon marked the course of a meandering stream and The Kid had been glad of the chance to turn Blizzard's head toward it. Horse and rider, framed in the intense blue of the western sky, formed a picture of beauty and grace as they drummed through the unmarked wastes. The Kid, riding "light" in his saddle, his supple body rising and falling with the rhythm of his loping mount and yet firm in his seat, dominated that picture. His face was tanned to the color of the buckskin shirt he wore, and a vast experience, born of hardship and danger on desert and mountain, was in his eyes—eyes that were sometimes gray and sometimes steely blue. Just now they were as carefree as the skies above.

A stranger might have wondered just what Kid Wolf's business was. He did not appear to be a cow-puncher, or a trapper or an army scout. A reata was coiled at his saddle, and two big Colts swung from a beaded Indian belt. No matter how curious the stranger might be, he would have thought twice before asking questions.

The horse, in color like snow with the sun on it, was splitting the breeze—and yet the stride was easy and tireless. Blizzard, big and immensely strong, was as fast as the winds that swept the Panhandle.

The stream, Kid Wolf discovered, was a fairly large creek bordered with a wild tangle of bushes, vines, and creeper-infested trees. It was no easy matter to force one's way through the choked growth, especially without making a great deal of noise.

But The Kid never believed in advertising his presence unnecessarily. He had the uncanny Apache trick of slipping silently through underbrush, even while on horseback. The country of the Indian Nations, at that time, was a territory infested with peril. And even now, although he seemed to be alone on the prairie, he was cautious.

Some distance before he reached it, he saw the creek, swollen and brown from rains above. So quiet was his approach that even a water moccasin, sunning itself on the river bank, did not see him.

Suddenly the white horse pricked up its ears. Kid Wolf, too, had heard the sound, and he pulled up his mount to watch and listen, still as a statue.

Splash! Splash! A rider was bringing his horse down to the creek at a walk. The sounds came from above and from across the stream. The water on that side had overflowed its bank and lay across the sand in blue puddles. In a few minutes Kid Wolf caught sight of a man on a strawberry roan, coming at a leisurely gait. As it was a white man, and apparently a cattleman, The Kid's vigilance relaxed a little.

In another moment, though, his heart gave a jump. And then, even before his quick muscles could act in time to save the newcomer it had happened. From behind a bush clump, a figure had popped up, rifle leveled. A thin jet of flame spat out of the rusty gun barrel, followed by a cracking report and a little burst of steaming smoke.

The man on the strawberry roan lurched wildly, groaned, and pitched headlong from his saddle, landing in the creek edge with a loud splash. One foot still stuck in a stirrup, and for a few yards the frightened pony dragged him through the muddied water. Then something gave way, and the murdered man plumped into the water and disappeared.

The killer stood on his feet, upright. He laughed—a chilling, mirthless rattle—and began to reload his old-pattern rifle. He was a half-breed Indian. The dying sun glistened on his coppery, strongly muscled flesh, for he was stripped to the waist. He wore trousers and a hat, but his hair hung nearly to his shoulders in a coarse snarl, and his feet were shod with dirty moccasins.

Kid Wolf's eyes crackled. He had seen deliberate

61

murder committed, an unsuspecting man shot down from ambush. His voice rang out:

"Drop that rifle and put up yo' hands!"

The soft drawl of the South was in his accents, but there was nothing soft about his tone. The half-breed whirled about, then slowly loosened his hold on his gun. It thudded to the grass. On a line with his bare chest was one of Kid Wolf's big-framed .45s.

The snaky eyes of the half-breed were filled with panic, but as The Kid did not shoot or seem to be about to do so, they began to glitter with mockery. Kid Wolf dismounted, keeping his gun leveled.

"Why did yo' shoot that man?" he demanded.

The half-breed was sullenly silent for a long moment. "What yuh do about it?" he sneered finally.

Kid Wolf's smile was deadly. His answer took the murderer by surprise. The half-breed suddenly found his throat grasped in a grip of steel. The fingers tightened relentlessly. The Indian's beady eyes began to bulge; his tongue protruded. With all his strength he struggled, but Kid Wolf handled him with one arm, as easily as if he had been a child!

"Yo're goin' to answer fo' yo' crime—that's what I'm goin' to do about it!" The Kid declared.

The half-breed's yell was wild and unearthly, when the grip at his throat was released. All the fight was taken out of him. Kid Wolf shook him until his teeth rattled, picked him up bodily and hurled him across his saddle.

"I'm takin' yo' to the law," he drawled. "I might kill

yo' now and be justified, too. But I believe in doin' things in the right way."

At the mention of "law," the half-breed snarled contemptuously.

"Ain't no law," he grunted, "southwest o' Dodge. Yuh no take me there. Too far."

Kid Wolf knew that the killer was right. Still, on the prairie, men make their own commandments.

"Theah's a new town, I hear, not far from heah—Midway, I think they call it," he drawled. "Yo're goin' theah with me, and if theah's no law in Midway, I'll see that some laws are passed. And yo' won't need that, eithah!" he added suddenly.

The knife that the half-breed had attempted to draw tinkled to the ground as The Kid gave the treacherous wrist a quick twist.

"Step along, Blizzahd," sang out Kid Wolf in his Southern drawl. "Back to the trail, as soon as we get a drink of watah, then no'th!"

At the mention of Midway, the half-breed's expression had changed to one of snakelike cunning. But if The Kid noted his half-concealed smile, he paid no attention to it. They were soon on their way.

Always, even in the savage lands beyond civilization, Kid Wolf tried to take sides with the weak against the strong, with the right against the wrong. And on more than one occasion he had found himself in hot water because of it.

The average man of the plains, upon seeing the murder committed, would have considered it none of

63

his business, and would have let well enough alone. Another type would have killed the half-breed on general principles. Kid Wolf however, determined that the murderer would be given a fair trial and then punished.

Again striking the Chisholm Trail—a well-beaten road several hundred yards wide—he veered north. Thousands upon thousands of longhorns from Texas and New Mexico had beaten that trail. This was the halfway point. Kid Wolf had heard of a new settlement in the vicinity, and, judging from the landmarks, he estimated it to be only a few miles distant.

In the meantime, the sun went down, creeping over the level horizon to leave the world in shadows which gradually deepened into dusk. All the while, the half-breed maintained a stoical silence. Kid Wolf, keeping a careful eye on him, but ignoring him otherwise, hummed a fragment of song:

"Oh, theah's hombres poison mean, on the Rio!
And theah's deadly men at Dodge, no'th o' Rio!
And to-day, from what I've seen,
Theah's some bad ones in between,
And I aim to keep it clean, beyond the Rio!"

Stars began to twinkle cheerily in the black vault overhead. Then The Kid made out a few points of yellow light on the plain ahead of them.

"That must be Midway," he mused to himself. "Those aren't stahs, or camp fiahs. Oil lamps mean a settlement."

64

Camps of any size were few and far between on the old Chisholm Trail. The moon was creeping up as Kid Wolf and his prisoner arrived, and by its light, as well as the few lights of the town, he could see that the word "town" flattered the place known as "Midway."

There were a few scattered sod houses, and on the one street were two large buildings, facing each other on opposite sides of the road. The first was a saloon, brilliantly lighted in comparison to the semidarkness of the other, which seemed to be a general store. A sign above it read:

THE IDEL HOUR SALOONE

Below it, in similar letters, the following was spelled out, or rather misspelled:

JACK HARDY
OWNER AND PROPRIATER

As the only life of Midway seemed to be centered here, Kid Wolf drew up his horse, Blizzard, dismounted, and dragged his prisoner to the swinging green doors that opened into the Idle Hour Saloon.

Pushing the half-breed through by main strength, he found himself in a big room, lighted by three oil lamps and reflectors suspended from beams in the roof. For all the haze of tobacco smoke, the place was agleam with light. For a moment Kid Wolf stood still in astonishment.

To find such a group of men together at one place, and especially such a remote place, was surprising. A score or more of booted-and-spurred loungers were at the bar and at the gambling tables. A roulette wheel was spinning at full clip, its little ivory ball dancing merrily, and at other tables were layouts of faro and various games of chance. Cards were being riffled briskly at a poker game near the door, and a little knot of men were in a corner playing California Jack.

Kid Wolf took in these details at a glance. What puzzled him was that these men did not appear to be cattlemen or followers of any calling, unless possibly it was the profession of the six-gun. All were heavily armed, and although that fact in itself was by no means unusual, The Kid did not like the looks of several of the men he saw there. Some were half-breeds of his prisoner's own stripe.

At The Kid's entrance with his still-struggling prisoner, every one stared. The bartender—a bulky fellow with a scarred face—paused in the act of pouring a drink, his eyes widening. The quiet shuffle of cards ceased, the wheel of fortune slowed to a clicking stop, and every one looked up in sudden silence.

Kid Wolf dragged the half-breed to the center of the room, holding him by the scruff of the neck.

"Men," he said quietly, "this man is a murderah!" In a few more words, he told the gathering what had happened.

From the very first, something seemed to warn The Kid of approaching trouble. Was it his imagination, or was a look flashed between the half-breed and several of the men in the room? He sensed an alert tenseness in the faces of those who were listening. One of the men, whom the Kid immediately put down as the owner of the saloon—Jack Hardy—was staring insolently.

Hardy was flashily dressed, wearing fancy-stitched riding boots, a fancy vest, and a short black coat, under which peeped the butt of a silver-mounted .44. Kid Wolf's intuition told him that he was the man he must eventually deal with.

The saloon owner had been watching the faro game. Now, having heard Kid Wolf out, he turned his back and deliberately faced the layout again.

"Go on with the game," he sneered to the dealer.

There was a world of contempt in his silky voice, and Kid Wolf flushed under his tan. Hardy pretended to ignore the visitor completely. The faro dealer slid one card and then another from his box; the case keeper moved a button or two on his rack. Then the dealer raked in the winnings from the losers. The game was going on as usual. The gamblers, taking their cue from Jack Hardy, turned to their games again. It was as if Kid Wolf had never existed.

The Kid took a firmer hold on the wriggling half-breed. "Do yo' know this man?" he demanded of the proprietor.

Hardy turned in annoyance, his black brows elevated sarcastically.

"It's 'Tucumcari Pete,'" he mocked. "What is it to yuh?"

Looking at the faro lookout, perched on his high stool, he winked. The lookout returned it knowingly.

Kid Wolf's eyes blazed. He had told his story so that all could hear. None had paid it any attention. All these men, then, were dishonest and unfriendly toward law and order.

"I want yo' to understand me," he said in a voice he tried to make patient. "This hombre—Tucumcari Pete, yo've called him—shot and killed a man from ambush. Isn't there any law heah?"

With long, tapered fingers, Jack Hardy rolled a cigarette, placed it between his lips and leered insultingly.

"There's only one law in Midway," he laughed evilly, "and that law is that all strangers must attend to their own business. Now I don't know who yuh are, but—"

"I'm Kid Wolf," came the soft-spoken drawl, "from Texas. My enemies usually call me by mah last name."

A man brushed near the Kid; his eye caught the Texan's significantly. But instead of speaking, he merely thrust a wadded cigarette paper in the Kid's hand as he passed by. So quickly was it done that nobody, it seemed just then, had seen the movement. Kid Wolf's heart gave a little leap. There was some mystery here! If he had made a friend, was that friend afraid to speak to him? Was there a note in that paper ball?

Hardy's eyes met the Texan's. They were insect eyes, beady and glittering black.

"All right," he snarled. "Mr. Wolf, you clear out!"

The Texan's fiery Southern temper had reached its

breaking point. It snapped. In a twinkling, things were happening. Using quick, almost superhuman strength, he picked up the half-breed by the neck and one leg and hurled him, like a thunderbolt, into the group at the faro table!

Tucumcari Pete's wild yell was drowned out by the tremendous crash of splintering wood and thudding flesh, as the half-breed's body hurtled through the air to smash Jack Hardy down to the floor with the impact.

The table went into kindling wood; chips and markers flew! A chair banged against the lookout's high perch, just as he was bringing his sawed-off shotgun to his shoulder.

Br-r-r-ram, bang! The double charge went into the ceiling, as the lookout toppled to the floor to join his companions, now a mass of waving arms and legs.

Kid Wolf's twin .45s had come out as if by magic. He ducked low. He did not need eyes in the back of his head to know that the men at the bar would open fire at the drop of the hat! A bullet winged venomously over him. Another one whined three inches from his ear. At the same instant, a bottle, hurled by the bartender, smashed to fragments against the wall.

But with one quick spring, Kid Wolf had his back against the green-shuttered door. For the first time, his Colts splattered red flame and smoke. There were three distinct reports, but they came so rapidly that they blended into one sullen, ear-shattering roar. He had aimed at the swinging lamps, and they went out so quickly that it seemed they had been extinguished by the force of one giant breath. Glass tinkled on the saloon floor, and all was wrapped in darkness. The Texan's voice rang out like the clang of steel on granite:

"Yo're goin' to have law! Kid Wolf law—and yo' may not like it as well as the othah kind!"

A score of revolver slugs, aimed at the sound of his voice, sent showers of splinters flying from the green-shuttered doors. The Texan, though, had taken care not to remain in the line of fire.

When the inmates of the Idle Hour swarmed out, looking for vengeance, they were disappointed. Kid Wolf and his horse, Blizzard, were nowhere to be seen!

CHAPTER VII

MCCAY'S RECRUIT

The Texan, after circling the town of Midway, rode in again. It was not his way to leave a job unfinished, with only a threat behind. The cigarette-paper note had aroused his curiosity to a fever heat. He read it by the light of the moon. It consisted of three pencil-scrawled words:

GO CROSS STREET

Across the wide street from the saloon, there was but one building. Was it here that he was to go? Was it a trap of some kind? He dismissed the latter possibility and decided to go at once to the big frame general store, using all the caution possible.

Approaching the place from behind, he looked it over carefully before dismounting. As Blizzard was conspicuous in the moonlight, he left him in a thick clump of bushes and slipped through the shadows on foot. As he neared the building, he discovered that it was not merely of frame, as he had at first thought. The boards in front masked a fortress of logs. It was so planned that a handful of defenders might hold it against great odds.

As Kid Wolf knocked softly on the rear door, he wondered if it had been built merely as a security against the renegade Indians, or for some other and deeper purpose. For a few minutes after he knocked, there was silence, then the door slowly opened. The Texan found himself looking into the barrel of a .45!

"What do yuh want here?"

Framed in the doorway, the Kid saw a grim young face glaring at him over the sights of the six-gun.

"Speak quick!" said the voice again.

"I will," the Texan said, "if yo'll kindly take that .45 out of my eye. I can talk bettah when I'm not usin' yo' gun barrel fo' a telescope."

"That gun," said the other sharply, "is goin' to stay just where I've got it!"

But it didn't. Kid Wolf's left hand snapped up under the gun and rapped smartly at just the right spot the wrist that held it. It was a trick blow—one that paralyzed the nerves for a second. The Colt dropped from the boy's quickly extended fingers and fell neatly into

Kid Wolf's right hand! All had happened so quickly that the youth hadn't time to squeeze the trigger. Before the amazed young man could recover himself, the Texan handed over the gun, butt first.

"Here yo' are," he drawled humorously. "To show yo' I mean well, I'm givin' it back. I do wish, though, that yo'd kindly point it some other way while I'm talkin'.""

The manner of the other changed at this. After losing his gun, he had expected a quick bullet.

"Guess yo're all right," he grinned slowly. "Come on in."

Passing through the door, Kid Wolf noted the thick loophole-pierced walls and other provisions for defense. Rifles stood on their stocks at intervals, ready to be snatched up at a moment's notice.

"Oh, dad!" the youth called in a low voice, as they entered the big main room of the building.

Six men were in the place, and The Kid took stock of them with one appraising glance. Although just as heavily armed as the faction across the street in the Idle Hour had been, they were of a different type. They were cattlemen, some old, some young. All looked up, startled. One of them got to his feet. He was a huge man and very fat. His face was round and good-humored, although his puckered blue eyes told of force and character.

"What's the matter, 'Tip'?" he asked of Kid Wolf's escort. "Who is this man?"

The Texan smiled and bowed courteously. "Maybe I should explain, sah," he drawled. "And aftah I'm done, perhaps yo'll have some information to give me."

He began his story, but was soon interrupted by an exclamation of anger and grief from the boy's father.

"A man on a strawberry roan, yuh say? And murdered! Why, that was Hodgson—one of my best men! Go on, young man! Go on with yore story!"

In a few words, the Texan told of bringing the halfbreed to the saloon across the street, and of his reception there.

"They-all told me to cleah out," he finished whimsically, "so I cleahed out the Idle Hour. Or rathah, I got the job started. Some one theah," he added, "handed me this note. That's why I'm heah."

The big man looked at it, and his face lighted.

"A short fella gave yuh that? I thought so! That was George Durham—one o' my men. He's there as a spy."

"As a spy?" the Texan repeated blankly. "I'm afraid this is gettin' too deep fo' me, Mistah—"

"McCay is the name. 'Old Beef' McCay, they call me," he chuckled. "This lad, yuh've already met. He's Tip McCay, and my son. And you?"

"Kid Wolf, sah, from Texas—just 'Kid' to my friends."

The five punchers, who had been listening with intense interest to the Texan's story, came forward to shake hands. They were introduced as Caldwell, Anderson, Blake, Terry White, and "Scotty." All were keen-eyed, resolute men.

"Now I'll tell yuh what this is all about," said the elder McCay. "When I spoke of a spy, I meant that

73

Durham is there to see if he can find out why Jack Hardy has imported those gunmen, and what he plans to do. Yuh see, I'm a cattle buyer. At this halfway point I buy lots o' herds from owners who don't wish to drive 'em through to Dodge. Then I sell 'em there at a profit—when I can."

"And Jack Hahdy?" drawled the Texan.

"Hardy is nothin' more or less than a cattle rustler— a dealer in stolen herds on a large scale. He's swore to get me, at the time when it'll do him the most good. In other words, at the time when he can get the most loot.

"So far," McCay went on, "there's been no bloodshed. Today it seems he's had Hodgson murdered. Looks as if things are about ripe for war!"

"He seems to have mo' men than yo'," murmured Kid Wolf.

"Yuh don't know the half of it. A dozen more of his hired gunmen rode south on the Chisholm Trail this mornin'."

"What does that signify?"

"Plenty," McCay explained. "Six o' my men are drivin' fifteen hundred steers up this way. Quite a haul, yuh see, for Hardy. They're due here tonight. If they don't get here—" The big man's wide mouth hardened.

"But I'm afraid I'm a poor host," he added apologetically. "Yuh'll have supper and stay the night with us, I'm sure. Tip, you an' Scotty go out and bring in The Kid's hoss."

The Texan consented, thanking him, and all began to make preparations for the night. The big general store

74

seemed more like a fort in time of war than anything else. Some of the men slept on the counters in the main room. A place was made for Kid Wolf in the rear. Sentries were on watch during the entire night, which passed uneventfully.

In the morning, just as the dawn was glowing in the east, the Texan was awakened by a horrified cry. All rushed to the front windows. Across the wide street, over the Idle Hour Saloon, a man was dangling, suspended from the roof by a rope! It was Durham—the man who had given Kid Wolf the cigarette-paper note. Some one had seen him in the act, and the fiends had lynched him.

"That settles it," said Kid Wolf grimly, turning to McCay. "I reckon I'm throwin' in with yo'. My guns are at yo' service!"

It was a situation not uncommon in that wilderness where "the law isn't, and the six-shooter is." Kid Wolf, however, had never seen a bolder attempt to trample on the rights of honest men. His veins beat hot at the thought of it. And Jack Hardy seemed to have the power to see it through to its murderous end.

It was not long after the discovery of Durham's murder when Tip McCay brought in a new note that had been pinned to the door.

"It was put there durin' the night some time, probably by one o' Hardy's sneakin' half-breeds, because none o' our sentries saw any one the whole night through," Tip said.

The note was roughly penciled on a sheet of yellow paper, and the message it carried was significant:

Ef yu will all walk out of their without yore guns we promiss no harm will com to yu. Ef yuh dont, we will get yu to the last man. We alreddy got yore cattel. This offer dont go fer Kid Wolf. We no hes their and we aim to kill him!

"They don't like me." The Texan laughed. "Well, I don't want 'em to. What do yo' intend to do, sah?"

The elder McCay's face was very red. His fingers, as he tore the insolent letter to bits, were trembling with anger.

"I say let 'em hop to it!" he jerked out. "I ain't givin' in to anybody!"

The others cheered. And it was a fighting group of men who gathered for a conference as to the defense of the store. It was agreed that their position was a serious one, outnumbered as they were.

Just how serious, they soon found out, for at the rising of the sun—as if it had been a signal—a burst of gunfire blazed out from the saloon across the street. Splinters flew from the logs as bullets thudded into them. Several whined through the two windows and crashed into the wall.

Kid Wolf took an active part in quickly getting ready for a stand. The windows and the doors were heavily barricaded, at his suggestion. Sacks of flour, salt, and other supplies were piled over the openings, as these were best for stopping lead. Mattresses were stuffed behind the barricade for further protection, and just enough space was left clear to allow a gun to be aimed through.

The volley from the Idle Hour had injured no one. The firing continued more or less steadily, however, and an occasional slug ripped its way between the logs. Jack Hardy's gang were firing at the chinks.

Up until this time, the defenders had not fired a shot. Even now, after the preparations had been made, Kid Wolf advised against wasting ammunition. The rustler gang were firing from the cover of the saloon, and were well protected.

"Hunt up all the guns heah," the Kid cried, "and load 'em. If they rush us, we'll need to shoot fast!"

Several rifles were hunted up—Winchesters and two muzzle-loading Sharps .50s. There were also a powder-and-ball buffalo gun of the old pattern, and, to Kid Wolf's delight, a sawed-off, double-barreled shotgun.

In the light of the early morning, each detail of the grim scene was brought out minutely. It was a picture Kid Wolf never forgot! Across the street that formed the No Man's Land was the saloon, wreathed in powder smoke, as guns spat sullen flame. And swinging slightly above the splintered green-shuttered doors was the dead body of Durham, neck stretched horribly, head on breast. It seemed a grotesque phantom, warning them of death to come.

The horses had been run into the back of the store

itself, as a protection against flying bullets. Kid Wolf suggested that they be saddled, so that they would be ready for use if occasion demanded it.

"We might have to make a run fo' it at any time," he warned.

The firing from the saloon went on for nearly an hour. Then there was a sudden lull.

"Look out now!" The Kid exclaimed. "Looks like they mean to rush us!"

"We'll cure 'em o' that!" Old Beef McCay cried grimly. He picked up the sawed-off shotgun.

The Texan was right. A yell went up from the saloon, and a dozen men rushed out, firing as they came. Six others carried a heavy beam, evidently torn from the interior of the Idle Hour. It was their intention to use this as a battering-ram to smash in the door of the store.

The cry from the defenders was "Let 'em have it!"

The terrific thunder of the shotgun and the buffalo rifle blended with the loud roar of six-guns. Hammers fell with deadly regularity. Fire blazed from every loophole and shooting space.

When the smoke cleared away, Tip McCay emitted a whoop that the others echoed. The charge had been stopped, and very effectively. The big beam lay on the ground, with the writhing bodies of four men around it. The "scatter gun" had accounted for three of them; Kid Wolf had put the other out of business with bullets through both legs. A little to one side were two more of the outlaws, one of whom had been brought down by

Tip McCay, the other by the lantern-jawed, slow-spoken plainsman known as Scotty. The others had beaten a quick retreat to the shelter of the saloon.

CHAPTER VIII

ONE GAME HOMBRE

Hardy's gang did not attempt another rush. They had learned their lesson. Keeping under cover, they continued firing steadily, however, and their bullets began to do damage. Every crack and chink was a target.

In the afternoon, more riders arrived to swell the Hardy faction. Some were ugly, half-clothed Indians, armed with rusty guns and bows and arrows. The odds were steadily increasing.

As there was ample food and water in the storehouse to last for several days, the besieged had no worries on that score. McCay knew, though, and Kid Wolf realized, that nightfall would bring trouble. Hardy was stung now by the loss of several men, and he would not do things by halves. He would show no mercy.

The first casualty took place in midafternoon. Anderson, in the act of aiming his revolver through a loophole, was hit between the eyes by a bullet and instantly killed. The number of men defending the store was now cut down to seven.

Toward nightfall, tragedy overtook them, full force.

Old Beef McCay was in the act of reloading a gun when a treacherous bullet zipped spitefully through an opening between two logs and caught him low in the chest. The impact sent him staggering against the wall, his round, moonlike face white and drawn.

"Dad!" called out Tip, in an agony of grief.

He and Kid Wolf rushed to the wounded man, supporting his great weight as it slowly sagged.

"Got me—son!" the cattleman jerked out.

Quickly the Texan tore away his shirt. He did not have to examine the wound to see how deadly it was; one glance was enough. Shot a few inches under the heart, McCay was dying on his feet.

"I'm done—all right," he grunted. "Listen, Tip. And you, Kid Wolf. I know yo're a true-blue friend. I want yuh to recover those cattle, if yuh ever get out of here alive. Yuh promise to try?" He turned glazing eyes at the Texan. "The cattle should go—to Tip's mother. She's in Dodge City."

"Believe me, sah," promised Kid Wolf earnestly, "if we evah get out of this trap alive, Tip and I will do ouah best."

The stricken man's face lighted. He grasped his son, Tip, with one hand, the Texan with the other.

"I'll pass on easier now."

Suddenly he drew himself up to his full height of well over six feet, squared his enormous shoulders, and with crimson welling from his wound, walked firmly and steadily to the door and began kicking the barricade aside.

"What are yuh doin'?" one of the defenders cried, thinking he was delirious from his hurt.

McCay, fighting against the weakness that threatened to overcome him, turned with a smile, grim and terrible.

"I'm goin' out there," he said, "to take some of those devils—with me!"

In vain Kid Wolf and Tip attempted to restrain him. The old man waved them back.

"I'm done for, anyway," he said. "I haven't got ten minutes to live. What if they do fill me with lead? I'll get one or two while they're doin' it!"

He seemed stronger now than ever. Sheer will power was keeping him on his feet. Seizing two revolvers, one in each big fist, he wabbled through the door.

With horror-widened eyes, they watched his reeling progress. He faltered to the hitch rack with bullets humming all around him. He clung to it for a moment, then went on, stalking toward the Idle Hour like grim vengeance! His guns sputtered red fire and bursts of black powder smoke. Hit time after time—they could see the dust fly from his clothing as he staggered along under the dreadful impacts—he kept going. It was glorious, terrible!

Tip hid his eyes, with a despairing cry. Kid Wolf watched, his face white under his sunburn.

Up to the very door of the Hardy refuge, the old man walked, his guns hammering claps of thunder. Hit several times in the body, he sprawled once and fell, but was on his feet again before the smoke drifted away. He plunged through the door, and The Kid saw two men drop under his blazing guns. Then McCay, too, fell—for the last time.

"Yo' dad was one game hombre, Tip," murmured the Texan, putting a comforting hand on the boy's shoulder. "Let's hope that when ouah turn comes, we can go as bravely."

He had never seen such an exhibition of undaunted courage. Although the tragedy had clutched at his heart, the spectacle had thrilled him, too. He knew that if he should escape, he would do his best to make good his promise to Old Beef McCay!

The McCay store was surrounded on all sides, and its four walls were scarred and pitted with bullet holes. And night was coming on rapidly. Kid Wolf saw the peril of their position. He knew, only too well, that the darkness would add to their troubles.

Twilight was deepening into dusk. Soon it became dark, and the moon would not be up for an hour. Kid Wolf, Tip McCay, and their four companions were never more alert. But even their keen eyes could not watch everything.

Young McCay was very pale. His father's death had touched him deeply, and fury against his killers burned in his glance. The others, too, were grim, thinking not of their own peril, but of the murderous Hardy gang. Thirsty for vengeance, they kept their eyes glued to their peepholes, fingers on gun triggers.

Tip had found a friend in Kid Wolf. No words were

wasted on sympathy now, or regrets, but Tip knew that the drawling Texan understood.

There was little shooting being done now, and the suspense was telling on the nerves of all of them. What was Hardy up to? Would he again attempt to batter down the door and force a way in, under cover of darkness this time? But they were not left long in doubt.

"I smell smoke!" cried Blake.

Immediately afterward a sharp, crackling sound came to their ears. Hardy's gang had set fire to the store! Under cover of darkness, one of the slinking Indians had crept up and ignited a pile of oil-soaked rags against the logs of the building. The flames rose high, licking hungrily upward.

"Get water!" some one shouted.

A bucketful or two from their supply tossed accurately through a loophole by Kid Wolf extinguished the blaze before it could rise higher. It was a close call, and it showed them what to expect now. The Indian's mistake had been in setting his fire where it could be reached by the defenders.

"We were pretty blamed lucky," Caldwell began. "If thet fire—"

"Not so lucky," sang out the Texan. "Look at *that!*"

From the direction of the saloon, a half dozen streaks of flame shot up into the sky like so many rockets. Fire whistled in the wind. The streaks were burning arrows, fired by Hardy's red-skinned cutthroats!

"That settles it!" groaned Tip resignedly. "They're fallin' on the roof!"

It was a wonder Hardy's evil brain hadn't thought of it before. Possibly some of his savage recruits had suggested it. At any rate, it was more to the rustler chief's purpose than smashing in the door. It would soon be all over for the defenders now.

In a breath, the roof was afire. Little jets of smoke began to spurt down from the beams over their heads, and the flames were fanned into a roar by the wind. Desperately the little handful of fighters exchanged glances. Things looked black indeed. They could not remain long in the burning death trap, and outside was Hardy's gang, waiting in the darkness to shoot them down if they ventured to escape.

"Steady, boys!" encouraged the Texan. "Theah may be a chance fo' us yet."

But one of them—Blake—was overcome with terror. In spite of what the others did to restrain him, he ran outside, tearing his way through the barricade. His hands were raised wildly over his head in token of surrender. But that made no difference to Hardy. There was a dull *spat,* and Blake went sprawling, shot through the heart.

"I hope nobody else tries that," drawled The Kid. "When we go, let's go togethah. By the light of this fiah they can see the colah of ouah eyes. We haven't a chance in the world to escape that way."

"We can't stay here and burn to death!" groaned Terry White.

The heat and smoke were driving them out of the main room. Already flames were creeping down the

84

walls, and the air was as hot as the breath of an oven. Their faces were blistered, their exposed hands cooked. Tip's coat was afire, as all five of them made a dash for the smaller room, taking the extra guns and ammunition with them.

This gave them a short respite. As yet the fire had not reached this apartment, although it would not take long. The smoke was soon so thick as nearly to be blinding. Stationing themselves at the loopholes, they began to work havoc with their rifles and revolvers. For the outlaws, bolder now, had ventured closer and made good targets in the glare of the burning building.

Suddenly there was a tremendous crash. The roof over the main room had come smashing in! Instantly the fire roared louder; tongues of it began to lick through the walls. Wood popped, and the heat became maddening. One side of the room became a mass of flames. The imprisoned men began to wet their clothing with the little water that was left.

"The stable!" ordered Kid Wolf. "Quick!"

The stable was built against the side of the store in the rear, and a door of the smaller room opened into it. There they must make their last stand.

The horses—and among them was Kid Wolf's white charger, Blizzard—were trembling with fear. They seemed to know, as well as their masters, that they were in terrible danger.

"We'll make ouah getaway with 'em, when the time comes," drawled the Texan.

"Not a chance in the world, Kid!" Tip groaned.

"Just leave it to me," was the quiet reply. "We've got a slim chance, if mah idea works."

Fanned by the wind, the flames soon were eating at the stable. And once caught, it burned like tinder. The horses screamed as the fire licked at them, and all was confusion. To make matters worse, bullets ripped through continually.

The Hardy band had gathered about the burning buildings in a close ring, ready to shoot down any one the instant he showed himself. The situation looked hopeless.

"Stay in there if yuh want to!" a voice shouted outside. "Burn up, or take lead! It's all the same to us!"

The heat-tortured Scotty staggered to his feet and groped toward one of the plunging, screaming horses.

"Lead is the easiest way," he choked. "They'll get me, but I'm goin' to try and ride this hoss out o' here!"

"Wait a minute!" Kid Wolf cried. "All get yo' hosses ready and make the break when I say the word. But not until!"

Gritting their teeth, they prepared to endure the baking heat for a few minutes more. They did not know what Kid Wolf was going to do, but they had faith that he would do something. And they knew, as things stood, that they could not hope for anything but death if they tried to escape now.

The stable was a mass of flames. The walls were crumbling and falling in. The Texan gave his final orders.

"If any of us get through," he gasped, "we'll meet on

the Chisholm Trail—below heah. Ride hard, with heads low—when I say the word!"

Then Kid Wolf played his trump card. Upon leaving the store itself, he had taken a small keg with him—a powder keg. Until now, none of the others had noticed it. Holding it in his two hands, he darted through the door into the open! Bits of burning wood were all about him; flames licked at his boots as he stood upright, the keg over his head.

"Scattah!" he shouted at the astonished Hardy gang. "I'm blowin' us all to kingdom come!"

The Texan made a glorious picture as he stood there, framed in red and yellow. Fire was under his feet and on every side. The glow of it illuminated his face, which was stained with powder smoke and blackened by the flames. His eyes shone joyously, and a laugh of defiance and recklessness was on his lips as he swung the poised keg aloft.

The Hardy gang, frozen with terror for an instant, scattered. They ran like frightened jack rabbits. To shoot Kid Wolf would have been easy, but none of them dared to attempt it. For if the keg was dropped, one spark would set it off. Overcome with panic, the ring of outlaws melted into the night.

The Texan gave the signal, and Tip, Caldwell, Scotty, and White tore out of the doorway on their frightened horses, heads low, scattering as they came. Kid Wolf whistled sharply for Blizzard and pulled himself effortlessly into the saddle as the big white horse went by at a mad gallop. He tossed away the keg as he did so.

The Hardy faction began shooting then, but it was too late. Bullets hummed over the heads of the escaping riders, but not one found its mark.

Kid Wolf found himself riding alongside Tip McCay. The others had taken different routes. The sounds of guns behind them were rapidly growing fainter, and they were hidden by the pitch darkness. Kid Wolf heard Tip laughing to himself—a rather high-pitched, nervous laugh.

"Are yo' all right, Tip?" sang out the Texan.

"Great! Yore plan worked to a T! But do yuh know what was in that powder keg yuh used?"

"Yes, I knew all the time," chuckled The Kid. "It wasn't powdah at all. It was lime. I found that out when I tried to load a Sharps rifle from it. But just the same, Tip, the bluff worked!"

CHAPTER IX

THE NIGHT HERD

By the time the Hardy faction had given up the chase in disgust, Caldwell, White, and Scotty had joined Tip and the Texan some miles below Midway on the Chisholm Trail. The former three were jubilant over their unexpected release from the fire trap, but they agreed with the Texan's first proposal.

"We've got mo' work to do, boys," he drawled. "If we wanted to, we could give that gang the slip fo' good and make ouah getaway. I think, though, that yo' feel as I do. What do yo' say we rustle back that herd o' long-horns that Hardy stole from Tip's dad?"

It meant running into danger again, and lots of it, but none of them hesitated. Kid Wolf had made his promise, and the others vowed to see him through. It took them but a few moments to plan their reckless venture and get into action.

The Kid hated Hardy now, just as heartily as did Tip McCay. And even if he had not given his word to the dying cattleman, he would not have left a stone unturned to bring the rustling saloon keeper to justice. More than once before, Kid Wolf had used the law of the Colt when other measures failed to punish. And now, even although handicapped and outnumbered, he planned to strike. The stolen herd represented a small fortune, and rightfully belonged to Tip McCay and his mother. But where were the longhorns now?

Tip's suggestion was helpful. He thought the cattle could not be more than a few miles below. They quickly decided to ride south, and Tip and The Kid led the way. The moon was up now, and it lighted the open prairie with a soft glow. The five riders pounded down the old Chisholm cattle road at a furious clip, eyes open for signs. Presently Tip cried:

"We'll find 'em down there at Green Springs! I see a light! It's a camp fire!"

On the horizon they made out the feathery tops of trees against the sky, and riding closer, they could see a dark mass bunched up around them—little dots straying out at the edges. It was the stolen McCay herd!

No general on the field of battle planned more carefully than the Texan. The party came closer, warily and making no noise. As they did so, they could hear the bawling of the cattle. Some were milling and restless, and the cattleman could see four men on horses at different points, attempting to keep the animals quiet and soothed. At the camp fire, several hundred yards from the springs, were four other men. Two of these seemed to be asleep in their blankets; the other pair were talking and smoking.

"The odds," drawled Kid Wolf in a low tone, "are eight to five in theah favah. Tip, yo' take the man on the no'th. Scotty, yores is the hombre on the west, ridin' the pinto. Caldwell, take the south man, and yo', White, do yo' best with the gent ovah east."

"How about those four by the fire?" whispered White.

"I'm takin' them myself." The Texan smiled. "We must all work togethah. They won't know who we are at first, probably, and will think we're moah of Hardy's men. Don't shoot unless yo' have to."

One of the two bearded ruffians by the camp fire clutched his companion's sleeve. Two other men lay snoring on the other side of the crackling embers, and one of them stirred slightly.

"Bill," he muttered, "didn't yuh hear somethin'?"

"I hear a lot o' cows bawlin'." The other grinned.

"But what I was tryin' to say is this: If Jack Hardy splits reasonable with us, why we—"

He was interrupted. Both men glanced up, to see a tall figure sauntering toward them into the ring of red firelight. Both stared, then reached for their guns.

"Sorry, gents," they were told in a soft and musical drawl, "but yo're a little late. Will yo' kindly poke yo' hands into the atmospheah?"

The two outlaws experienced a sudden wilting of their gun arms. It was quick death to attempt to draw while the round black eyes of this stranger's twin Colts were on them.

With a jerk, both threw up their hands. One gave a shout—a cry meant to warn his companions.

A shot from the direction of the herd told them, however, that the other outlaws were already aware of something unusual.

The two bandits in the blankets jumped up, rubbing their eyes in amazement. A kick from Kid Wolf's boot sent the .45 of one of them flying. The other, prodded none too gently with a revolver barrel, decided to surrender without further ado.

Lining them up, The Kid disarmed them. He was joined in a few minutes by Tip, White, Caldwell, and Scotty, who were driving two prisoners before them.

"*Bueno!*" said The Kid. "I see yo' got the job done without much trouble. But wheah's the othah two?"

Scotty smiled grimly, spat in the direction of the fire and said simply:

"They showed fight."

In five minutes, the six outlaws were tied securely with lariat rope, in spite of their fervent and profane protests.

"Jack Hardy will get yuh fer this, blast yuh!" snarled one.

"Maybe," drawled The Kid sweetly, "he won't want us aftah he gets us."

They planned to have the cattle moving northward by dawn. Once past Midway, the trail to Dodge was clear. But there was plenty of work to do in the meantime.

An hour after sunup, the herd of fifteen hundred steers was moving northward toward Midway. Kid Wolf and his four riders had them well under control, and had it not been for a certain alertness in their bearing, one would have thought it an ordinary cattle drive.

Kid Wolf was singing to the longhorns in a half-mocking, drawling tenor, as he rode slowly along:

"Oh, the desaht winds are blowin', on the Rio!
And we'd like to be a-goin', back to Rio!
　　But befo' we do,
　　We've got to see this through,
Like all good hombres do, from the Rio!"

The prisoners had been lashed securely to their horses and brought along. Already several miles had been traveled. And thus far the party had seen no signs of Jack Hardy's rustler gang. They were not, however, deceived. With every passing minute they were approaching closer to Midway, the Hardy stronghold. And not only that, but the outlaws were probably combing the country for them.

Reaching a place known as Stone Corral, they were especially vigilant. The place was a natural trap. It had been built of roughly piled stone and never entirely finished. Indians sometimes camped within the enclosure. It was, however, empty of life, and the adventurers were about to push on with the herd when the keen, roving eyes of Kid Wolf spotted something suspicious on the north horizon. He held his hand aloft, signaling a stop.

"Heah they come, boys!" he cried. "We'll have to stand 'em off heah!"

They had been expecting it, and they were hardly surprised or unprepared. They were favored, too, in having such a place for defense. Save for the low walls of the abandoned corral, there was no cover worth mentioning for miles. Among the cool-eyed five who prepared to make their stand, there was not one who hadn't faced death before and often. But never had the odds been more against them. They had slipped through the toils before, but now they were tightening again.

Watching the riders as they grew larger against the sky, they could count two dozen of them. There was no use to hide. They could not conceal the cattle herd, and the Hardy gang would surely investigate. Already they were veering in their course, riding directly toward the stone corral.

"Aweel," muttered Scotty, lapsing into his Scotch dialect for the moment, "there isn't mooch doot about how this thing will end. But I'm a-theenkin' we'll make it a wee bit hot for 'em before they get us!"

"Right yuh are, Scotty," said Tip savagely. "I'm goin' to try and pick Hardy out o' that gang o' killers, and if I do, I don't care much then what happens."

The prisoners had been herded within the corral, and their feet were lashed together.

"Yuh'll soon be listenin' to bullets," Caldwell told them. "Yuh'd better pray that yore pals shoot straight and don't hit you by mistake."

The Hardy gang had seen them! They saw the riders check their horses and then spread out in a cautious circle.

"Hardy ain't with 'em," sang out White, who had sharp eyes.

"They seem to be all there but him!" snapped Tip in disappointment. "The coward's stayed behind!"

A bullet suddenly buzzed viciously over the corral and kicked up a shower of clods behind it. And as if this first shot were signal, a shattering volley rang out from the oncoming riders. Bits of stone and bursts of sand flew up from the low stone breastworks.

"We got yuh this time!" one of the rustlers shouted. "We're givin' yuh one chance to come out o' there!"

"And we're givin' yuh all the chances yo' want," replied Kid Wolf, "to come and get us!"

For answer, the horsemen—two dozen strong— charged! In a breath, they had struck and had been driven back. So quickly had it happened that nobody remembered afterward just how it had been done. The Texan's two Colts grew hot and cooled again. Three riderless horses galloped about the corral in circles, and the thing was over!

It had been sheer nerve and courage against odds, however. Three of the attackers fell from their horses before the stone walls had been gained, and three others had met with swift trouble inside. The rest had retreated hastily, leaving six dead and wounded behind. Only Caldwell had been hit, and his wound was a slight one in the shoulder. The defenders cheered lustily.

"Come on!" Tip shouted. "We're waitin'!"

Kid Wolf, however, was not deceived. The attacking party was made up largely of half-breeds and Indians. The Texan knew their ways. That first charge had been only half-hearted. The next time, the outlaws would fight to a finish, angered as they were to a fever heat. And although the defenders might account for a few more of the renegades, the end was inevitable. Kid Wolf did not lose his cool smile. He had been in tight situations before, and had long ago resigned himself to dying, when his time came, in action.

"Here they come again!" barked Scotty grimly.

But suddenly a burst of rifle fire rang out in the distance—a sharp, crackling volley. Two of the outlaw gang dropped. One horse screamed and fell heavily with its rider.

The five defenders saw to their utter amazement that a large band of horsemen was riding in from the east at a hot gallop, guns spitting fire. As a rescue, it was timed perfectly. The rustlers had been about to charge the corral, and now they reined up in panic, undecided what to do. Two others fell. And in the meantime, the new-comers, whoever they were, were circling so as to sur-round them on all sides.

"It's the law!" Kid Wolf smiled.

"The what?" Caldwell demanded. "Why, there ain't no law between here an'—"

But the Texan knew he was right. He had seen the sun glittering on the silver badge that one of the strange riders wore.

The rustlers themselves were outnumbered now. The posse included a score of men, and they handled their guns in a determined way. The outlaws fired a wild shot or two, then signified their surrender by throwing up their hands. While the sullen renegades were being searched and disarmed, the leader of the posse came over to where the Texan and the others were watching.

"Who in blazes are you?" he shot out.

"That's the question I was goin' to ask yo', sheriff," returned The Kid politely.

"Humph! How d'ye know I'm a sheriff?" grunted the leader.

"Yo're wearin' yore stah in plain sight."

"Oh!" The officer grinned. "Well, I'm Sheriff Dawson, o' Limpin Buffalo County. I've brought my posse over two hundred miles to get my hands on one o' the worst gangs o' rustlers in the Injun Nations. I don't know who you are, but the fact that yuh were fightin' 'em is enough fer me. I know yo're all right."

"Thanks, sheriff," said the Texan. "I'm leavin' Mr. Tip McCay heah to tell yo' ouah story, if yo'll excuse me fo' a while."

"Where yuh goin', Kid?" demanded young McCay, astonished.

"To Midway," drawled the Texan, swinging himself into Blizzard's saddle. "Looks like a clean sweep has been made of the Hahdy gang—except Hahdy himself. I reckon I'll ride in and get him, so's to make the pahty complete."

"Hardy!" the officer ejaculated. "I want that *malo hombre*—and mighty bad, dead or alive!"

"Let us go along!" burst out Tip.

"No," laughed the Texan quietly. "Yo' boys have had enough dangah and excitement fo' one day, not includin' yestahday. I'd rathah settle this little business with Jack Hahdy alone. Yo' drive the cattle on and meet me latah."

And lifting his hand in farewell, The Kid touched his white charger with the spur. In a few minutes he was a tiny spot on the horizon, bound for the lair of Jack Hardy, the rustler king.

There was one thing, however, that Kid Wolf was not aware of, and that was a pair of beady black eyes watching him from behind a prairie-dog hill! One of the renegade half-breeds had managed to slip away from the posse unseen. It was Tucumcari Pete, and in a draw a few yards away was his pony.

CHAPTER X

TUCUMCARI'S HAND

Jack Hardy was annoyed. He had planned carefully, expecting to have no difficulty in wiping out the hated McCays and those who sympathized with them.

His plans had only partially succeeded. The elder McCay was dead, but Tip and some of the others had slipped through his clutches. To have the McCay faction wiped out of Midway forever meant money and power to him. And now his job was only half finished.

"They'll get 'em," he muttered to himself.

He was alone in his place, the Idle Hour. He had sent every available man, even his bartender, out on the chase. He wanted to finish, at all costs, what he had begun.

"It was all due to that blasted hombre from Texas!" he groaned. "I wish I had him here, curse him! It would've all gone smooth enough if he hadn't meddled. Well, he'll pay! The boys will get him. And when they do—" Hardy thumped the bar with his fist in fury.

He paced the floor angrily. The deserted building seemed to be getting on his nerves, for he went behind the bar several times and, with shaking fingers, poured stiff drinks of red whisky. Then he walked to one of the deserted card tables and began to riffle the cards aimlessly.

There were two reasons why the rustling saloon keeper had not joined in the search for his victims. One was that he hated to leave unprotected the big safe in his office, which always contained a snug sum of money. The other was that Jack Hardy was none too brave when it came to gun fighting. He was still seated at the card table, laying out a game of solitaire, when the swinging doors of the saloon opened quietly. The first inkling Hardy had of a stranger's presence, however, was the soft drawl of a familiar voice:

"Good mohnin', Mistah Hahdy! Enjoyin' a little game o' cahds?"

Hardy's body remained stiff and rigid for a breathless moment, frozen with surprise. Then he turned his head, and his right hand moved snakelike downward. Just a few inches it moved, then it stopped. Hardy had thought he had a chance, and then he suddenly decided that he hadn't. At his first glance, he had seen Kid Wolf's hands carelessly at his sides; at his second, he saw them holding two .45s!

Kid Wolf's smile was mocking as he sauntered into the room. His thumbs were caressing the gun hammers.

"No, it wouldn't be best," he drawled, "to monkey with that gun o' yo'n. They say, yo' know, that guns are dangerous because they go off. But the really dangerous guns are those that don't go off quick enough."

The rustler leader rose to his feet on shaking legs. His face had paled to the color of paper, and beads of perspiration stood out on his pasty forehead.

"Yuh—yuh got the drop, Mr. Wolf," he pleaded. "Don't kill me!"

"Nevah mind," the Texan said softly. "When yo' die, it'll be on a rope. It's been waitin' fo' yo' a long time. But now I have some business with yo'. First thing, yo'd bettah let me keep that gun o' yo'n"

The Kid pulled Hardy's .44 from its holster beneath the saloon man's black coat.

"Next thing," he drawled, "I want yo' to take that body down from in front o' yo' do'."

Kid Wolf referred to the corpse of the unfortunate McCay spy whom Hardy had hanged. It still hung outside the Idle Hour, blocking the door.

The Texan made him get a box, stand on it and loosen the rope from the dead man's neck. Released from the noose, the body sagged to the ground.

"Just leave the noose theah," ordered The Kid. "It may be that the sheriff will have some use fo' it."

"The sheriff!" Hardy repeated blankly.

"Yes, he'll be heah soon," murmured Kid Wolf softly. "I have some business with yo' first. Maybe we'd bettah go to yo' office."

Jack Hardy's office was a little back room, divided off from the main one of the Idle Hour. In spite of his protests, Hardy was compelled to unlock this apartment and enter with his captor.

"Tip has recovahed his fathah's cattle," The Kid told him pointedly, "but theah's the little mattah of the burned sto' to pay fo'. In behalf of Tip and his mothah,

I'm demandin'—well, I think ten thousand dollahs in cash will just about covah it."

"I haven't got ten thousand!" Hardy began to whine.

But The Kid cut him off. "Open that safe," he snapped, "and we'll see!"

Hardy took one look at his captor and decided to obey and to lose no time in doing so. The Texan's eyes were crackling gray-blue.

A large sheaf of bills was in an inner drawer, along with a canvas bag of gold coins. Ordering Hardy to take a chair opposite, Kid Wolf began to count the money carefully. To allow himself the free use of his hands, he holstered both his guns.

"When this little mattah is settled," the Texan drawled, "I have a little personal business with yo', man to man."

Jack Hardy moistened his lips feverishly. Although he was not now covered by The Kid's guns, he lacked the courage to begin a fight. He knew how quick Kid Wolf could be, and he was a coward.

The Texan was stacking the gold into neat piles.

"Fo'teen thousand two hundred dollahs," he announced finally. "The odd fo' thousand two hundred will go to the families of the men yo' murdahed yestahday. And now, Mistah Jack Hahdy, my personal business with yo' will be—"

He did not finish. The door of the little office had suddenly opened, and Tucumcari Pete stood in the entrance! His evil face was gloating, his snaky eyes glittering with the prospect of quick revenge. In his dirty hands was a rifle, and he was raising it to cover The Kid's heart!

Kid Wolf's hands were on the table. There was no time for him to draw his Colts! It seemed that the half-breed had taken a hand in the game and that he held the winning cards! In a second it would be over. The half-breed's finger was reaching for the trigger; his mouth was twisted into a gloating, vicious smile.

But while The Kid was seated in such a position at the table that he could not hope to reach his guns quickly enough, he had his hole card—the bowie knife in a sheath concealed inside his shirt collar. The Kid could draw and hurl, if necessary, that gleaming blade as rapidly as he could pull his 45s. His hand darted up and back. Something glittered in the air for just a breath, and there was a singing *twang!*

Tucumcari Pete gasped. His weird cry ended in a gurgle. He lowered his rifle and teetered on his feet. The flying knife had found its mark—the half-breed's throat! The keen-pointed blade had buried itself nearly to the guard! Clawing at the steel, Tucumcari staggered, then dropped to the floor with his clattering rifle. His body jerked for a moment, then stiffened. Justice had dealt with a murderer.

"The thirteenth ace," The Kid drawled softly, "is always in the deck!"

But Hardy had taken advantage of Tucumcari's interruption. Jumping up with an oath, he hurled the table over upon The Kid and leaped for the door. The Texan scrambled from under the heavy table and darted after him. Hardy was running for his life. He raced into the main room of the Idle Hour with The Kid at his heels.

Kid Wolf could have drawn his guns and shot him down. But it was too easy. Unless forced to do so, that was not the Texan's way.

Snatching open a drawer in one of the gambling tables, Hardy seized a large-bore derringer and whirled it up to shoot. But The Kid's steel fingers closed on his wrist. The ugly little pistol exploded into the ceiling— once, and then the other barrel.

"There'll be no guns used!" said The Kid, with a deadly smile. "I told yo' we'd have this out man to man!"

Hardy's lips writhed back in a snarl of hatred. He sent a smashing right-hand jab at the Texan's heart. Kid Wolf blocked it, stepped to one side and lashed the rustler king under the eye. Hardy staggered back against the table, clutching it for support. The Kid pressed closer, and Hardy dodged around the table, placing it between him and his enemy. The Texan hurled it to one side and smashed his way through the saloon owner's guard.

Hardy, head down to escape The Kid's terrific blows, bucked ahead with all his power and weight advantage and seized him about the waist. It was apparent that he was trying to get his hands on one of the Texan's guns. At close range, Kid Wolf smashed at him with both hands, his fists smacking in sharp hooks that landed on both sides of Hardy's jaw. To save himself, Hardy staggered back, only to receive a mighty blow in the face.

"I'll kill yuh for that, blast yuh!" he cried with a snarl.

Hardy was strong and heavy, but the punishment he was receiving was telling on him. His breath was coming in jerky gasps. Seizing the high lookout stool from the faro layout, he advanced toward The Kid, his eyes glittering with fury.

"I'll pound yore head to pieces!" he rasped.

"Pound away," Kid Wolf said.

Hardy whirled it over his head. Kid Wolf, however, instead of jumping backward to avoid it, darted in like a wild cat. While the stool was still at the apex of its swing, he struck, with the strength of his shoulder behind the blow. It landed full on the rustler's jaw, and Hardy went crashing backward, heels over head, landing on the wreckage of the stool. For a moment he lay there, stunned.

"Get up!" snapped The Kid crisply. "Theah's still mo' comin' to yo'."

Staggering to his feet, Hardy made a run for the front door. Kid Wolf, however, met him. Putting all the power of his lean young muscles behind his sledgelike fists, he hit Hardy twice. The first blow stopped Hardy, straightened him up with a jolt and placed him in position for the second one—a right-hand uppercut. *Smash!* It landed squarely on the point of Hardy's weak chin. The blow was enough to fell an ox, and the rustler chief went hurtling through the door, carried off his feet completely.

What happened then was one of those ironies of fate. The rope on which Hardy had hanged the McCay spy, George Durham, still hung before the door, its noose swaying in the wind some five feet from the ground. Hardy hit it. His head struck the rope with terrific force—caught in the loop for an instant. There was a sharp snap, and Hardy dropped to the wooden sidewalk. For a few moments, his body twitched spasmodically, then lay still and rigid. His neck had been broken by the shock!

For a minute Kid Wolf stared in unbelief. Then he smiled grimly.

"Guess I was right," he murmured, "when I said it was on the books fo' Hahdy to die by the rope!"

Cattle were approaching Midway on the Chisholm Trail—hundreds of them, bawling, milling, and pounding dust clouds into the air with their sharp hoofs.

The Texan, watching the dark-red mass of them, smiled. McCay cattle, those! And there was a woman in Dodge City who was cared for now—Tip's mother.

"I guess we've got the job done, Blizzard." He smiled at the big white horse that was standing at the hitch rack. "Heah comes the boys!"

It was a wondering group that gathered, a few minutes later, in the ill-fated Idle Hour. They listened in amazement to Kid Wolf's recital of what had taken place since he left them.

"And so Hardy hanged himself!" the sheriff from Limping Buffalo ejaculated, when he could find his voice. "Well, I must say that saves me the trouble o' doin' it! But there's some reward comin' to yuh, Mr. Wolf."

The Texan smiled. "Divide it between Scotty, Caldwell, and White," he drawled. "And, Tip, heah's the ten thousand Mistah Hahdy donated. Present it to yo' good mothah, son, with mah compliments."

Tip could not speak for a minute, and when he did try to talk, his voice was choked with emotion.

"I can't begin to thank yuh," he said.

Kid Wolf shook his head. "Please don't thank me, Tip. Yo' see, I always try to make the troubles of the undah dawg, mah troubles. So long as theah are unfohtunates and downtrodden folks in this world, I'll have mah work cut out. I am, yo' might say, a soldier of misfohtune."

"But yo're not goin'?" Tip cried, seeing the Texan swing himself into his saddle.

"I'm just a rollin' stone—usually a-rollin' toward trouble," said the Texan. "Some time, perhaps, we'll meet again. Adios!"

Kid Wolf swung his hat aloft, and he and his white horse soon blurred into a moving dot on the far sweeps of the Chisholm Trail.

CHAPTER XI

A BUCKSHOT GREETING

"Oh, the cows stampede on the Rio Grande!
    The Rio!
The sands do blow, and the winds do wail,
But I want to be wheah the cactus stands!
And the rattlah shakes his ornery tail!"

K id Wolf sang his favorite verse to his favorite tune, and was happy. For he was on his beloved Rio.

He had left the Chisholm Trail behind him, and now "The Rollin' Stone" was rolling homeward, and—toward trouble.

The Kid, mildly curious, had been watching a certain dust cloud for half an hour. At first he had thought it only a whirling dervish—one of those restless columns of sand that continually shift over the arid lands. But it was following the course of the trail below him on the desert—rounding each bend and twist of it.

The Texan, astride his big white horse, had been "hitting the high places only," riding directly south at an easy clip, but scorning the trail whenever a short cut presented itself.

Descending from the higher ground of the mesa now, by means of an arroyo leading steeply down upon the plain, he saw what was kicking up the dust. It was a buckboard, drawn by a two-horse team, and traveling directly toward him at a hot clip. There was one person, as far as he could see, in the wagon. And across this person's knees was a shotgun. The Kid saw that unless he changed his course he would meet the buckboard and its passenger face to face.

Kid Wolf had no intention of avoiding the meeting, but something in the tenseness of the figure on the seat of the vehicle, even at that distance, caused his gray-blue eyes to pucker.

The distance between him and the buckboard rapidly decreased as Kid Wolf's white horse drummed down between the chocolate-colored walls of the arroyo. Between him and the team on the trail now was only a stretch of level white sand, dotted here and there with low burrow weeds. Suddenly, the driver of the buckboard whirled the shotgun. The double barrels swung up on a line with Kid Wolf.

Quick as the movement was, the Texan had learned to expect the unexpected. In the West, things happened, and one sought the reason for them afterward. His hands went lightning-fast toward the twin .45s that hung at his hips.

But Kid Wolf did not draw. A look of amazement had crossed his sunburned face and he removed his hands from his gun butts. Instead of firing on the figure in the buckboard, Kid Wolf wheeled his horse about quickly, and turned sidewise in his saddle in order to make as small a target as possible.

The shotgun roared. Spurts of sand were flecked up all around The Kid and the big white horse winced and jumped as a ball smashed the saddletree a glancing blow. Another slug went through the Texan's hat brim. Fortunately, he was not yet within effective range.

Even now, Kid Wolf did not draw his weapons. And he did not beat a retreat. Instead, he rode directly toward the buckboard. The click of a gun hammer did not stop him. One barrel of the shotgun remained unfired and its muzzle had him covered.

But the Texan approached recklessly. He had doffed his big hat and now he made a courteous, sweeping bow. He pulled his horse to a halt not ten yards from the menacing shotgun.

"Pahdon me, ma'am," he drawled, "but is theah anything I can do fo' yo', aside from bein' a tahget in yo' gun practice?"

The figure in the buckboard was that of a woman! There was a moment's breathless pause.

"There's nine buckshot in the other barrel," said a feminine voice—a voice that for all its courage faltered a little.

"Please don't waste them on me," Kid Wolf returned, in his soft, Southern speech. "I'm afraid yo' have made a mistake. I can see that yo' are in trouble. May I help yo'?"

Doubtfully, the woman lowered her weapon. She was middle-aged, kindly faced, and her eyes were swollen from weeping. She looked out of place with the shotgun—friendless and very much alone.

"I don't know whether to trust you or not," she said

wearily. "I suppose I ought to shoot you, but I can't, somehow."

"Well I'm glad yo' can't," drawled The Kid with contagious good humor. His face sobered. "Who do yo' think I am, ma'am?"

"I don't know," the woman sighed, "but you're an enemy. Every one in this cruel land is my enemy. You're an outlaw—and probably one of the murderers who killed my husband."

"Please believe that I'm not," the Texan told her earnestly. "I'm a strangah to this district. Won't yo' tell me yo' story? I want to help yo'."

"There isn't much to tell," the driver of the buckboard said in a quavering voice. "I'm on the way to town to sell the ranch—the S Bar. I have my husband's body with me on the wagon. He was murdered yesterday."

Not until then did Kid Wolf see the grim cargo of the buckboard. His face sobered and his eyes narrowed.

"Do yo' want to sell, ma'am?"

"No, but it's all I can do now," she said tearfully. "Major Stover, in San Felipe, offered me ten thousand for it, some time ago. It's worth more, but I guess this—this is the end. I don't know why I'm tellin' you all this, young man."

"This Majah Stovah—is he an army officer?" The Kid asked wonderingly.

The woman shook her head. "No. He isn't really a major. He never was in the army, so far as any one knows. He just fancies the title and calls himself 'Major Stover'—though he has no right to do so."

"A kind of four-flushin' hombre—a coyote in sheep's clothin', I should judge," drawled Kid Wolf.

"Thet just about describes him," the woman agreed.

"But yo' sho'ly aren't alone on yo' ranch. Wheah's yo' men?" asked The Kid.

"They quit last week."

"Quit?" The Kid's eyebrows went up a trifle.

"All of them—five in all, includin' the foreman. And soon afterward, all our cattle were chased off the ranch. Gone completely—six hundred head. Then yesterday"—she paused and her eyes filled with tears—"yesterday my husband was shot while he was standing at the edge of the corral. I don't know who did it."

No wonder this woman felt that every hand was turned against her. Kid Wolf's eyes blazed.

"Won't the law help yo'?" he demanded.

"There isn't any law," said the woman bitterly. "Now you understand why I fired at you. I was desperate—nearly frantic with grief. I hardly knew what I was doing."

"Well, just go back home to yo' ranch, ma'am. I don't think yo' need to sell it."

"But I can't run the S Bar alone!"

"Yo' won't have to. I'll bring yo' ridahs back. Will I find them in San Felipe?"

"I think so," said the woman, astonished. "But they won't come."

"Oh, yes, they will," said The Kid politely.

"But I can't ranch without cattle."

"I'll get them back fo' yo'."

111

"But they're over the line into Old Mexico by now!"

"Nevah yo' mind, ma'am. I'll soon have yo' place on a workin' basis again. Just give me the names of yo' ridahs and I'll do the rest."

"Well, there's Ed Mullhall, Dick Anton, Fred Wise, Frank Lathum, and the foreman—Steve Stacy. But, tell me, who are you—to do this for a stranger, a woman you've never seen before? I'm Mrs. Thomas."

The Texan bowed courteously.

"They call me Kid Wolf, ma'am," he replied. "Mah business is rightin' the wrongs of the weak and oppressed, when it's in mah power. Those who do the oppressin' usually learn to call me by mah last name. Now don't worry any mo', but just leave yo' troubles to me."

Mrs. Thomas smiled, too. She dried her eyes and looked at the Texan gratefully.

"I've known you ten minutes," she said, "and somehow it seems ten years. I do trust you. But please don't get yourself in trouble on account of Ma Thomas. You don't know those men. This is a hard country—terribly hard."

Kid Wolf, however, only smiled at her warning. He remained just long enough to obtain two additional bits of information—the location of the S Bar and the distance to the town of San Felipe. Then he turned his horse's head about, and with a cheerful wave of his hand, struck out for the latter place. The last he saw of Mrs. Thomas, she was turning her team.

Kid Wolf realized that he had quite a problem on his

hands. The work ahead of him promised to be difficult, but, as usual, he had gone into it impulsively—and yet coolly.

"We've got a big ordah to fill, Blizzahd," he murmured, as his white horse swung into a long lope. "I hope we haven't promised too much."

He wondered if in his endeavor to cheer up the despondent woman he had aroused hopes that might not materialize. The plight of Mrs. Thomas had stirred him deeply. His pulses had raced with anger at her persecutors—whoever they were. His Southern chivalry, backed up by his own code—the code of the West—prompted him to promise what he had.

"A gentleman, Blizzahd," he mused, "couldn't do othahwise. We've got to see this thing through."

Ma Thomas—he had seen at a glance—was a plainswoman. Courage and character were in her kindly face. The Texan's heart had gone out to her in her trouble and need.

Once again he found himself in his native territory, but in a country gone strange to him. Ranchers and ranches had come in overnight, it seemed to him. A year or two can make a big difference in the West. Two years ago, Indians—today, cattle! Twenty miles below rolled the muddy Rio. It was Texas—stern, vast, mighty.

And, if what Mrs. Thomas had said was correct, law hadn't kept pace with the country's growth. There was no law. Kid Wolf knew what that meant. His face was very grim as he left the wagon trail behind.

The town of San Felipe—two dozen brown adobes, through which a solitary street threaded its way—sprawled in the bottom of a canyon near the Rio Grand. The cow camp had grown, in a few brief months, with all the rapidity of an agave plant, which adds five inches to its size in twenty-four hours. San Felipe was noisy and wide awake.

It was December. The sun, however, was warm overhead. The sky was cloudless and the distant range of low mountains stood out sharp and clear against the sky. As Kid Wolf rode into the town, a hard wind was blowing across the sands and it was high noon.

San Felipe's single street presented an interesting appearance. Most of the long, flat adobes were saloons—The Kid did not need to read the signs above them to see that. The loungers and hangers-on about their doors told the story. Sandwiched between two of the biggest bars, however, was a small shack—the only frame building in the place.

"Well, this Majah Stover hombre must be in the business," muttered The Kid to himself.

His eyes had fallen on the sign over the door:

MAJOR STOVER
LAND OFFICE

Kid Wolf was curious. Strange to say, he had been thinking of the major before he had observed the sign, and wondering about the man's offer to buy the S Bar Ranch. The Texan whistled softly as he dismounted. He

114

left Blizzard waiting at the hitch rack, and sauntered to the office door.

He opened the door, let himself in, and found himself in a dusty, paper-littered room. A few maps hung on the walls. Kid Wolf's first impression was the disagreeable smell of cigar stumps.

His eyes fell upon the man at the desk by the dirty window, and he experienced a sudden start—an uncomfortable feeling. The Texan did not often dislike a man at first sight, but he was a keen reader of character.

"Do yuh have business with me?" demanded the man at the desk.

Major Stover, if this were he, was a paunchy, disgustingly fat man. His face was moonlike, sensually thick of lip. His eyes, as they fell upon his visitor, were hoglike, nearly buried in sallow folds of skin. The thick brows above them had grown close together.

"Well," The Kid drawled, "I don't exactly know. Yo' deal in lands, I believe?"

"I have some holdings," said the fat man complacently. "Are yo' interested in the San Felipe district?"

"Very much," said The Kid, nodding. "I am quite attracted by Rattlesnake County, and—"

"This isn't Rattlesnake County, young man," corrected the land agent. "This is San Felipe County."

"Oh, excuse me," murmured the Texan, "maybe I got that idea because of the lahge numbah of snakes—"

"There's no more snakes here than—" the other began.

"I meant the human kind," explained Kid Wolf mildly.

Major Stover's eyes narrowed suspiciously. "What do yuh want with me?" he demanded.

"Did yo' offah ten thousand dollahs fo' the S Bar Ranch?"

"That is none of yore business!"

"No?" drawled Kid Wolf patiently. "Yo' might say that I am heah as Mrs. Thomas' agent."

The major looked startled. "Where's yore credentials?" he snapped, after a brief pause.

Kid Wolf merely smiled and tapped the butts of his six-guns. "Heah, sah," he murmured. "I'm askin' yo'."

Major Stover looked angry. "Yes," he said sharply, "I did at one time make such an offer. However, I have reconsidered. My price is now three thousand dollars."

"May I ask," spoke The Kid softly, "why yo' have reduced yo' offah?"

"Because," said the land dealer, "she has to sell now! I've got her where I want her, and if yo're her agent, yuh can tell her that!"

One stride, and Kid Wolf had fat Major Stover by the neck. For all his weight, and in spite of his bulk, The Kid handled him as if he had been a child. An upward jerk dragged him from his chair. The Texan held him by one muscular hand.

"So yo' have her where yo' want her, have yo'?" he cried, giving the major a powerful shake.

He passed his other hand over the land agent's flabby body, poking the folds of fat here and there over Major

Stover's ribs. At each thump the major flinched.

"Why, yo're as soft as an ovahripe pumpkin," Kid Wolf drawled, deliberately insulting. "And yo' dare to tell me that! No, don't try that!"

Major Stover had attempted to draw an ugly-looking derringer. The Kid calmly took it away from him and threw it across the room. He shook the land agent until his teeth rattled like dice in a box.

"Mrs. Thomas' ranch, sah," he said crisply, "is not in the mahket!"

With that he hurled the major back into his chair. There was a crashing, rending sound as Stover's huge body struck it. The wood collapsed and the dazed land agent found himself sitting on the floor.

"I'll get yuh for this, blast yuh!" gasped the major, his bloated face red with rage. "Yo're goin' to get yores, d'ye hear! I've got power here, and yore life ain't worth a cent!"

"It's not in the mahket, eithah," the Texan drawled, as he strolled toward the door. At the threshold he paused.

"Yo've had yo' say, majah," he snapped, "and now I'll have mine. If I find that yo' are in any way responsible fo' the tragedies that have ovahtaken Mrs. Thomas, yo'd bettah see to yo' guns. Until then— adios!"

CHAPTER XII

THE S BAR SPREAD

The bartender of the La Plata Saloon put a bottle on the bar in front of the stranger, placing, with an added flourish, a thick-bottomed whisky glass beside it. This done, he examined the newcomer with an attentive eye, pretending to polish the bar while doing so.

The man he observed was enough to attract any one's notice, even in the cosmopolitan cow town of San Felipe. Kid Wolf was worth a second glance always. The bartender saw a lean-waisted, broad-shouldered young man whose face was tanned so dark as to belie his rather long light hair. He wore a beautiful shirt of fringed buckskin, and his boots were embellished with the Lone Star of Texas, done in silver. Two single-action Colts of the old pattern swung low from his beaded belt.

"Excuse me, sir," said the bartender, "but yore drink?"

"Oh, yes," murmured The Kid, and placed a double eagle on the bar.

"No, yuh've already paid fer it." The bartender nodded at the whisky glass, still level full of the amber liquor. "I was just wonderin' why yuh didn't down it."

"Oh, yes," said Kid Wolf again. He picked up the glass between thumb and forefinger and deliberately emptied it into a handy cuspidor. "I leave that stuff to mah enemies," he said, smiling. "By the way, can yo' tell me where I can find a Mistah Mullhall, a Mistah Anton, a Mistah Lathum, a Mistah Wise, and a Mistah Steve Stacy?"

When the bartender could recover himself, he pointed out a table near the door.

"Wise an' Lathum an' Anton is right there—playin' monte," he said. "Stacy an' Mullhall was here this mornin', but I don't see 'em now."

Thanking him, Kid Wolf sauntered away from the bar and approached the gambling table.

The La Plata Saloon was fairly well patronized, even though it lacked several hours until nightfall. Kid Wolf had taken the measure of the loiterers at a glance. Most of them were desperadoes. "Outlaw" was written over their hard faces, and he wondered if Ma Thomas hadn't been right about the county's general lawlessness. San Felipe seemed to be well supplied with gunmen.

The three men at the table, although they were "heeled" with .45s, were of a different type. They were cowmen first, gunmen afterward. Two were in their twenties; the other was older.

"I beg yo' pahdon, caballeros," said The Kid softly, as he came up behind them, "but I wish to talk with yo' in private. Wheah can we go?"

There was something in the Texan's voice and bearing that prevented questions just then. The trio faced about in surprise. Plainly, they did not know whether to take Kid Wolf for a friend or for a foe. Like true Westerners, they were not averse to finding out.

"We can use the back room," said one. "Come on, you fellas."

One of them delayed to make a final bet in the game, then he followed. At a signal to the bartender, the back room, vacant, save for a dozen bottles, likewise empty, was thrown open to them.

"Have chairs, gentlemen," The Kid invited, as he carefully closed the door.

The trio took chairs about the table, looking questioningly at the stranger. The oldest of them picked up a deck of cards and began to shuffle them absently. Kid Wolf quietly took his place among the trio.

"Boys," he asked slowly, "do yuh want jobs?"

There was a pause, during which the three punchers exchanged glances.

"Lay yore cards face up, stranger," invited one of them. "We'll listen, anyway, but——"

"I want yo' to go to work fo' the S Bar," said The Kid crisply.

"That settles that," growled the oldest puncher, after sending a searching glance at the Texan's face. The others looked amazed. "No. We've quit the S Bar."

"Who suggested that yo' quit?" The Kid shot at them.

The man at the Texan's right flushed angrily. "I don't see that this is any of yore business, stranger," he barked.

"Men," said The Kid, and his voice was as chill as steel, "I'm makin' this my business! Yo're comin' back to work fo' the S Bar!"

"And yo're backin' thet statement up—how?"

120

demanded the oldest cow hand, suddenly ceasing to toy with the card deck.

"With these," returned Kid Wolf mildly.

The trio stared. The Kid had drawn his twin .45s and laid them on the table so quickly and so quietly that none of them had seen his arms move.

"Now, I hope," murmured The Kid, "that yo' rather listen to me talk than to those. I've only a few words to say. Boys, I was surprised. I didn't think yo' would be the kind to leave a po' woman like Mrs. Thomas in the lurch. Men who would do that, would do anything—would even run cattle into Mexico," he added significantly.

All three men flushed to the roots of their hair.

"Don't think we had anything to do with thet!" exclaimed one.

"We got a right to quit if we want to," put in the oldest with a defiant look.

"Boys, play square with me and yo' won't be sorry," Kid Wolf told them earnestly. "I know that all these things happened after yo' left. Since then, cattle have been rustled and Mr. Thomas has been murdahed—yo' know that as well as I do. That woman might be yo' mothah. She needs yo'. What's yo' verdict?"

There was a long silence. The three riders looked like small boys whose hands had been caught in the cooky jar.

"How much did Majah Stovah pay yo' to quit?" added the Texan suddenly.

The former S Bar men jumped nervously. The man at The Kid's left gulped.

"Well," he blurted, "we was only gettin' forty-five, and when Stover offered to double it, and with nothin' to do but lie around, why, we—"

"Things are changed now," said The Kid gently. "Ma Thomas is alone now."

"That's right," said the oldest awkwardly. "I suppose we ought to—"

"Ought to!" repeated one of the others, jumping to his feet. "By George, we will! I ain't the kind to go back on a woman like Mrs. Thomas. I don't care what yuh others do!"

"That's what I say," chorused his two companions in the same breath.

"I'll show yo' I aim to play fair," Kid Wolf approved. He took a handful of gold pieces from his pocket and placed them on the table in a little pile. "This is all I have, but Mrs. Thomas isn't in a position to pay right now, so heah is yo' first month's wages in advance."

The three looked at him and gulped. If ever three men were ashamed, they appeared to be. The old cow-puncher pushed the pile back to The Kid.

"We ain't takin' it," he mumbled. "Don't get us wrong, partner. We ain't thet kind. We never would've quit the S Bar if it hadn't been for Steve Stacy—the foreman. And, of course, things was goin' all right at the ranch then. Guess it's all our fault, and we're willin' to right it. We don't know yuh, but yo're O. K., son."

They shook hands warmly. The Kid learned that the oldest of the three was Anton. Wise was the bow-legged one, and Lathum was freckled and tall.

"Stacy hadn't better know about this," Lathum decided.

"I was hopin' to get him back," said The Kid.

"No chance. He's in with the major now," spoke up Wise. "So's Mullhall. Neither of 'em will listen—and they'll make trouble when they find we're goin' back."

"If yo'-all feel the same way as I do," Kid Wolf drawled as they filed out of the back room, "they won't have to make trouble. It'll be theah fo' 'em."

As they approached the bar, Anton clutched The Kid's elbow.

"There's Steve Stacy and Mullhall now," he warned in a low voice.

Stacy and Mullhall were big men, heavily built. Upon seeing the party emerge from the back room, they pushed away from the bar and came directly toward Kid Wolf, who was walking in the lead.

"Steve Stacy's the hombre in front," Wise whispered. "Be on yore guard."

The Kid knew the ex-foreman's type even before he spoke. He was the loud-mouthed and overbearing kind of waddy—a gunman first and a cowman afterward. His beefy face was flushed as red as his flannel shirt. His eyes were fixed boldly on the Texan.

"The barkeeper tells me yuh were inquirin' fer me," he said heavily. "What's on yore mind?"

Mullhall was directly behind him, insolent of face and bearing. The two seemed to be paying no attention to the trio of men behind The Kid.

"I was just goin' to offah yo' a chance to come back

to the S Bar," explained Kid Wolf. "These three caballeros have already signed the pay roll again.

It was putting up the issue squarely, with no hedging. Both Stacy and Mullhall darkened with fury.

"What's yore little game? I guess it's about time to put an extra spoke in yore wheel!" snarled Mullhall, coming forward.

"Who in blazes are you?" sneered Stacy.

"Just call me The Wolf!" The Kid barked. "I'm managin' the S Bar right now, and if yo' men don't want to be friends, I'll be right glad to have yo' fo' enemies!"

Mullhall had pressed very close. It was as if the whole thing had been prearranged. His hands suddenly shot out and seized Kid Wolf's arms—pinning them tightly.

It was an old and deadly trick. While Mullhall pinioned the Texan, Steve Stacy planned to draw and shoot him down. The pair had worked together like the cogwheels of a machine, and all was perfectly timed. Stacy drew like a flash, cocking his .45 as it left the holster.

The play, however, was not worked fast enough. Kid Wolf was not to be victimized by such a threadbare ruse. He was too fast, too strong. He whirled Mullhall about, his left boot went behind Mullhall's legs. With all his force he threw his weight against him, tearing his arms free.

Mullhall went backward like a catapult, directly at Stacy. The gun exploded in the air, and as the slug buzzed into the roof, both Mullhall and the ex-foreman went down like bags of meal—a tangled maze of legs and arms.

"Get up," The Kid drawled. "And get out!"

Kid Wolf had not bothered to draw his guns, but Anton, Wise, and Lathum had reached for theirs, and they had the angry pair covered. Stacy changed his mind about whirling his gun on his forefinger as he recovered it, and sullenly shoved it into its holster.

"We'll get yuh!" snarled Stacy, his furious eyes boring into The Kid's cool gray ones. "San Felipe is too small to hold both of us!"

"Bueno," said The Kid calmly. "I wish yo' luck— yo'll need it. But in the meantime—vamose pronto!"

Swearing angrily, the two men obeyed. It seemed the healthiest thing to do just then. They slunk out like whipped curs, but The Kid knew their breed. He would see them again.

> "Oh, the wintah's sun is shinin' on the Rio,
>   I'm ridin' in mah homeland and I find it
>   mighty nice;
> Life is big and fine and splendid on the Rio,
>   With just enough o' trouble fo' the spice!"

If Kid Wolf's improvised song was wanting from a poetical standpoint, the swinging, lilting manner in which he crooned it made up for its defects. His tenor rose to the canyon walls, rich and musical.

"Our cake's plumb liable to be overspiced with trouble," Frank Lathum said with a laugh.

Kid Wolf, with his three newly hired riders, were well on their way to the S Bar. His companions knew of a

125

short route that would take them directly to the Thomas hacienda, and they were following a steep-walled canyon out of the mesa lands to the westward.

"Look!" cried Wise. "Somebody's coming after us!"

They turned and saw a lone horseman riding toward them from the direction of San Felipe. The rider was astride a fast-pacing Indian pony and overhauling them rapidly. Since leaving the town, Kid Wolf's party had been in no hurry, and this had enabled the rider to over-take them.

"It's Goliday," muttered Anton, shading his weather-beaten eyes with a brown hand.

"Just who is he?" The Kid drawled.

"I think he's really the hombre behind Major Stover," Wise spoke up. "He owns the ranch to the north o' the S Bar, and from what I hear, Stover has been tryin' to buy it fer him."

"Oh," The Kid murmured, "let's wait fo' him then, and heah what he has to say."

Accordingly, the four men drew up to a halt and wheeled about to face the oncoming ranchman. They could see him raising his hand in a signal for them to halt. He came up in a cloud of dust, checked his pony, and surveyed the little party. His eyes at once sought out Kid Wolf.

Goliday was a man of forty, black-haired and sallow of face. He wore a black coat and vest over a light-gray shirt. Beneath the former peeped the ivory handle of a .45.

"Hello," panted the newcomer. "Are you the hombre

126

that caused all the stir back in San Felipe?"

"What can I do fo' yo'?" asked the Texan briefly.

"Well," said Goliday, "let's be friends. I'll be quite frank. I want the S Bar. Is it true yo're goin' there to run the place for the old woman?"

"It is," The Kid told him.

"I'll pay yuh well to let the place alone," offered Goliday after a pause. "I'll give five thousand cash for the ranch, and if the deal goes through, why I'm willin' to ante up another thousand to split between you four.

"I'm a generous man, and it'll pay to have me for a friend. Savvy? As an enemy I won't be so good. Now, Mr. Wolf, if that's yore name, just advise Mrs. Thomas to sell right away. Is it a bargain?"

"It's mo' than that," murmured The Kid softly. "It's an insult."

Goliday did not seem to hear this remark. He reached into his vest and drew out something that glittered in the sun.

"Here's a hundred and twenty to bind the bargain—six double eagles. And there's more where these came from. Will yuh take 'em?"

"I'll take 'em," drawled Kid Wolf. He reached out for the gold, and they clinked into his palm. "I'll take 'em," he repeated, "and heah's what I'll do with 'em!"

With a sweeping movement, he tossed them high into the air. The sun glittered on them as they went up. Then, with his other hand, The Kid drew one of his guns.

Before the handful of coins began to drop, The Kid was firing at them. He didn't waste a bullet. With each quick explosion a piece of gold flew off on a tangent. *Br-r-rang, cling! Br-r-rang, ting!* There were six coins, and The Kid fired six times. He never missed one! He picked the last one out of the air, three feet from the ground.

Goliday watched this exhibition of uncanny target practice with bulging eyes. As the echoes of the last shot died away, he turned on The Kid with a bellow of wrath.

"No, yo' don't!" Kid Wolf sang out.

Goliday took his hand away from the butt of his ivory-handled gun. The Texan had pulled his other revolver with the bewildering speed of a magician. Goliday was covered, "plumb center."

"That's our answah, sah!" The Kid snapped.

Goliday's sallow face was red with rage.

"I have power here!" he rasped. "And yuh'll hear from me! There's only one law in this country, and that's six-gun law—yuh'll feel it within forty-eight hours!"

"Is that so?" said The Kid contemptuously. "I have a couple of lawyahs heah that can talk as fast as any in San Felipe County. The S Bar accepts yo' challenge. Come on, boys. Let's don't waste any mo' time with this."

Grinning, the quartet struck out again westward, leaving the disgruntled ranchman behind. The last they saw of him, he was kicking about in the mesquite, looking for his gold.

CHAPTER XIII

DESPERATE MEASURES

Nightfall found the quartet established in the S Bar bunk house. The joyful thanks of Ma Thomas was enough reward for any of them. She hadn't expected to see Kid Wolf again, she said, and to have him return with help was a wonderful surprise.

She was a woman transformed and had taken new heart and courage. The supper she prepared for them, according to Kid Wolf, was the best he had eaten since he had left Texas.

All four of them were exceedingly hungry, and they made short work of Ma Thomas' enchiladas, crisp chicken *tacos,* peppers stuffed, and her marvelous *menudo—a* Mexican soup.

"With such eats as this," sighed The Kid, "I know the S Bar is saved."

They were gathered now in the long, whitewashed adobe bunk house, and had finished their sad task of burying Thomas, victim of an assassin's bullet.

The Kid obtained the bullet that had taken the old rancher's life. It was a .45 slug, and while the others believed it useless as evidence, The Kid carefully put it away in his pocket.

"It's hard to say who done it," Fred Wise said doubtfully.

"Yes," The Kid agreed. "I believe Ma Thomas was

right when she said the hand of every one in San Felipe seemed to be raised against her. How much do yo' suppose the S Bar is wo'th, Anton?"

"Well, with five good springs—two rock tanks and three gravel ones, she's a first-class layout. The pick of the country. I'd say twenty thousand."

"The robbers!" muttered Kid Wolf.

"What's on the program?" asked Frank Lathum. "We can't do much ranchin' without cattle."

"No," admitted The Kid. "We must get those cattle back."

"But who ever heard o' gettin' cattle out o' Old Mexico after they've once been driven in?" Anton growled. "It can't be done!"

"Money in cattle can't be hid like money in jewels or cash," said The Kid. "Theah not so easy to get rid of, even in Mexico. The town of Mariposa lies just over the bordah, am I right? And the only good cattle lands for a hundred miles are just south of theah, isn't that so?"

"Yes, but—"

"Men, this is a time fo' desperate measures. We must stake all on one turn of the cards. Boldness might win. I want yo' hombres to be in Mariposa the day *pasado mañana*."

"The day after tomorrow!" Wise repeated. "What's yore plan, Kid?"

"I don't know exactly," Kid Wolf admitted. "I make mah plans as I go along. But I'm ridin' into Mexico tomorrow to see what I can see. I'll try to have the six hundred head of S Bar cattle in Mariposa the next day, some way or anothah."

Bold was the word! The quartet talked until a late hour. The three riders had caught some of The Kid's own enthusiasm and courage.

"Ma Thomas sure needs us now," said Anton.

"Hasn't she any relatives?" Kid Wolf asked.

"A son," muttered Wise in a tone of disgust. "Small good he is."

"Where is he?"

"Nobody knows," growled Lathum. "Somewhere in Mexico, I guess. He was practically run out o' San Felipe. He's no *bueno.*"

Kid Wolf learned that the son—Harry Thomas—had nearly broken his parents' hearts. He had become wild years before, and was now nothing more or less than a gambler, suspected of being a cheat and a "short-card operator."

"He was a tinhorn, all right," said Wise, "and fer the life of me I don't know how a woman like Ma Thomas could have such a worthless rake fer a son. He was a queer-lookin' hombre—one brown eye and one black eye."

"Ma loves him, though. Yuh can tell thet," put in Lathum.

"Oh, yes," pointed out Anton soberly. "Mothers always do. Great things, these mothers."

He blew his nose violently on his red bandanna, and shortly afterward went to bed. Soon all four were in the bunks, resting for the hard work that awaited them on the morrow—mañana—and many days after mañana.

Kid Wolf was up very early the next morning, and saddled Blizzard after a hasty breakfast. He had much to do.

The three S Bar men went part way with him—to a point beyond the south corral. It was here that Mrs. Thomas had found the body of her murdered husband. There seemed to be no clue as to who had performed the deliberate killing. Before The Kid left, however, he did a little scouting around. In the sand behind a mesquite, fifty yards from the spot where the body had been found, he discovered significant marks.

"Come ovah heah, yo' men," he sang out.

Distinct in the sand were the prints made by a pair of low-heeled, square-toed boots.

"Well," Anton grunted.

"Know those mahks?"

All shook their heads. They had certainly been made by an unusual pair of boots. In a country where high-heeled riding footgear was the thing, such boots as these were seldom seen. All three admitted that they had seen such boots somewhere, but, although they racked their brains, they were unable to say just who had worn them.

"Well, take a good look at them," drawled The Kid. "I want yo' to be witnesses to the find. Some day this info'mation might be of use. In the meantime, adios, boys!"

"Good luck!" they shouted after him. "We'll be on hand at Mariposa mañana morning."

Kid Wolf hit the trail for Mexico at a hammer-and-tongs gallop.

The Mexican town of Mariposa was scattered over ten blazing acres of sand just south of the Rio Grande. It was an older city than San Felipe, and its buildings were more elaborate.

One in particular, just off the Plaza, attracted the eye of Spanish ranchman and peon alike. It was the meeting place of the thirsty—the famed El Chihuahense, a saloon and gambling house known from El Paso to California.

Built of brown adobe originally, it had been painted a bright red. The carved stone with which it was trimmed shone in white contrast to the vivid walls. An archway was the entrance to the establishment and many a bullet hole within its shadow testified to the dark deeds that had happened there.

Now, as on every night, the place was ablaze with light. Big oil lamps by the score, backed by polished reflectors, illumined the interior. From within came the strains of guitars and the gay scrapings of a fiddle, mingled with the hum of Spanish voices, an occasional oath in English, and the rattle of chips and coins.

At the hitch rack outside the saloon stood a big white horse—waiting.

Kid Wolf was playing poker in the El Chihuahense, and he had been at it for two solid hours. Those who knew The Kid better would have wondered at this. Ordinarily, Kid Wolf was not a gamester. He played

133

cards rarely, never for any personal gain, and only when there seemed to be a good reason for so doing. But the Texan knew the game.

A trio of Mexican landowners who thought they were skilled at it had quickly found out their error—and withdrew, more or less gracefully. Now a crowd of swarthy-faced men, numbering more than a score, were massed around the draw-poker table near the door. They were watching the masterful play of this slow-drawling hombre—this gringo stranger who had been seen about Mariposa all day, and who now was "bucking heads" with a lone antagonist.

Kid Wolf's opponent was also an American, but one well known to the Mariposans. A stack of gold coins was piled in front of him, and he riffled the cards as he dealt in the manner of a professional. This man was young, also. He wore a green eye shade, and a diamond glittered in his fancy shirt. He was a gambler.

The game seesawed for a time. First Kid Wolf would make a small winning, and then the man with the green eye shade. Most of the bets, however, were so heavy as to make the Mexicans about the table gasp with envy.

But the crisis was coming. The deal passed from the gambler to The Kid and back to the gambler again. The pot was already swollen from the antes. The Kid opened.

"I'm stayin'," said the gambler crisply. He pushed in a small pile of gold. "How many cards?"

"Two," murmured The Kid.

The gambler took one. The chances were, then, that

134

he had two pairs, or was drawing to make a flush or a straight.

Carefully the two men looked at their cards. Not a muscle of their faces twitched. The gambler's face was frozen—as expressionless as an Indian's. Kid Wolf was his easy self. His usual smile was very much in evidence, unchanged. He made a bet—a large one, and the gambler called and raised heavily. The Kid boosted it again. Then there was a silence, broken only by the tense breathing of the onlookers, who had pushed even closer about the table.

"Five hundred more," said the gambler after a nerve-racking pause.

"And five," The Kid drawled softly, pushing most of his gold into the center of the table.

The gambler's hand shook the merest trifle. Again he looked at the pasteboards in his pale hands. Then he quickly pushed every cent he had into the pot.

"I'm seeing it, and I'm elevatin' it every coin on me. It'll cost yuh—let's see—eight hundred and sixty more!"

It was more than the Texan had—by four hundred dollars. He could, however, stay for his stack. The man in the green eye shade could take out four hundred to even the bet. The Kid, though, did not do this.

"I'll just write an I O U fo' the balance," he drawled.

"But supposin' yore I O U ain't good?"

"Then this is good," said Kid Wolf.

The gambler stared. The Texan had placed a .45 on the table near his right hand. And it had been done so quickly that the onlookers exchanged glances. Who was this hombre?

"All right," growled the man in the green eye shade.

Kid Wolf wrote something with a pencil stub on a bit of paper. When finished, he tossed it to the center of the gold pile, carefully folded.

"That calls yo'," he said coolly. "What have yo'?"

Nervously, the gambler spread his hand face up on the table. His hands were shaking more than ever.

"A king full," he jerked out, wetting his lips.

Three kings and a pair of tens—a very good layout in a two-handed game with a huge pot at stake!

"Beats me," said The Kid. "I congratulate yo'."

With a sigh of relief, the gambler began to pull the winnings toward him.

"Better look at the I O U," The Kid drawled, "and see that it's all right and proper." As he spoke, he tossed his cards carelessly toward the gambler, face down.

The youth in the green eye shade unfolded the paper and looked at the writing within. His eyes widened a little and he looked again, blinking. Slowly the following words swam into his consciousness:

Son, you can't gamble worth a cent, but rake in the money and follow me in five minutes. I'll meet you back of the saloon. I'm your friend, Harry Thomas, and your mother's happiness is at stake.

The gambler's face went a bit paler. Only his poker face kept the astonishment out of his eyes. Slowly and

136

furtively he looked at the cards Kid Wolf had tossed away so carelessly. The Texan had held four aces!

CHAPTER XIV

AT DON FLORISTO'S

In the moonlight, behind the El Chihuahense Saloon, Kid Wolf and the gambler met. The latter found The Kid leaning silently against a ruined adobe wall in the deserted alleyway. The sound of the music from within the gambling hall could be heard faintly. There was a silence after the two men faced each other. Harry Thomas finally broke it:

"How did yuh know me? I go by the name of Phil Hall here. And who are yuh?"

"Just call me The Kid," was the soft answer. "I knew yo' by yo' one brown and one black eye."

"What did yore note mean?"

"Harry, the S Bar is in great danger. Yo' father is dead, and yo' mothah—" And then Kid Wolf told the story in full.

Harry Thomas listened in agitation. He was overcome with grief and remorse. His voice trembled when he spoke:

"I've been a fool," he blurted, "worse than a fool. Poor mother! What can I do now?"

"It isn't too late to help her," The Kid told him kindly. "Yo' mothah needs yo' badly. Findin' those stolen cattle wasn't so hahd, aftah all. Theah on Don Floristo's ranch just below heah. I've talked to the don, and let the remahk drop that I'm interested in cattle. So I am, but the don doesn't know in what way. He thinks I'm a rich gringo wantin' to buy some."

"Kid, I've learned my lesson. I'll never gamble again," said Harry earnestly.

Kid Wolf took his hand warmly.

"Don Floristo has already given orders that the six hundred head of S Bar steers are to be driven to Mariposa tonight. I am to ride south to his ranch and close the deal. Early mañana the three loyal S Bar men will seize the cattle and drive them home. Yo' and I must help."

"Yo're riskin' yore life for strangers, Kid. Floristo is a dyed-in-the-wool villain. If he suspects anything, he'll cut yore throat. But I'm with yuh! Yuh've brought me to myself. I didn't suppose they made hombres like you!"

"Thanks, Harry. Now listen carefully and I'll tell yo' exactly what to do."

For a few minutes The Kid talked earnestly to young Thomas, outlining their night's work. Then Kid Wolf took leave of the young man—slipping back through the shadows to the street again.

Harry Thomas walked quickly to the Establo—Mariposa's biggest livery stable. Kid Wolf mounted his horse Blizzard. He struck off through the town at an easy trot and headed southward through the darkness.

138

Don Manuel Floristo's rancho was the largest in that part of Mexico. Several thousand steers roamed his range—steers that for the most part bore doubtful brands. Don Floristo's reputation was not of the best. His rancho was suspected of being a mere trading ground for stolen herds. Rustlers from both sides of the line made his land their objective.

Kid Wolf had found the S Bar cattle easily enough. The brands had been gone over, being burned to an 8 Bar J. The work had been done so recently, however, that he was not deceived. He had called on the don and told him that he was "interested in cattle," which was true. The don's lust for gold had done the rest. He supposed that Kid Wolf was an American who desired to go into the ranching business near the boundary. A good chance to get rid of the "hot" herd of six hundred!

"Just the size of herd the señor needs to start," Floristo had said. "Six hundred head at ten pesos—six thousand pesos. Ees it not cheap, amigo?"

"Very cheap," The Kid had told him. "Now if these cattle were delivered at Mariposa—"

"Easy to say, but no harder to do, señor," was the don's eager reply. "I will give orders now to have them driven there. Do you wish to buy a ranch, señor? Or have you bought? Perhaps I could help."

"Perhaps. But I want cattle right now. I have friends just no'th of the bordah."

The don had smiled cunningly. This fool gringo would have trouble with those stolen cattle if he drove them back into the States. That, however, was no concern of Floristo's.

"Come back tonight, señor," he had begged.

And now The Kid was on his way to the don's hacienda. He had purposely timed his visit so that he would reach Floristo's rancho at a late hour. Already it was after midnight.

Blizzard was unusually full of spirit. The slow pace to which The Kid held him was hardly an outlet for his restless energy.

"Steady, boy," The Kid whispered. "We're savin' our strength—they'll be plenty of fast ridin' to do latah."

The Kid could not resist the temptation to break into song. His soft chant rose above the faint whisper of the desert wind:

"Oh, theah's jumpin' beans and six-guns south
    o' Rio,
    And *muy malo* hombres by the dozen,
We're a-watchin' out fo' trouble south o' Rio,
    And when it comes, some lead will be
    a-buzzin'."

He smiled up at the stars, and turned Blizzard's head to the eastward. Before them loomed the low, white adobe walls of Don Floristo's hacienda.

A dark-faced peon on guard outside, armed with a carbine, opened the door for him. Late as the hour was, lights were shining inside and he heard the welcoming sound of Don Floristo's voice as he passed through the entrance.

"Ah, come in, come in, amigo. I was afraid the señor was not coming. *Como esta usted?*"

"*Buenas noches,*" returned The Kid, with easy politeness. "I trust yo' are in good health?"

The conversation after that was entirely in Spanish, as Kid Wolf spoke the language like a native. His Southern accent made the Mexican tongue all the more musical. He followed his host into a rather large, square room with a beautifully tiled floor. The don motioned The Kid to a chair.

"The cattle of which we—ah—spoke, señor," said the don, as he lighted a long brown cigarette. "They are on the way to Mariposa. Are probably there even now, amigo."

"Yes?" drawled Kid Wolf.

"You will have men there to receive them?"

"Without fail," replied the Texan, a strange inflection in his tones.

"It is well, my friend. With the cattle are four of my men. They will not turn over the herd, of course, until"—he paused significantly—"the money is paid."

Kid Wolf smiled. He leaned back in his chair and crossed his legs.

"One does not pay for stolen cattle, Don Floristo," he drawled.

The muscles of the don's body stiffened. Kid Wolf's face was a smiling mask. The showdown had come.

There was a long pause. The Kid's arms were folded easily on his breast.

"Who are you?" the don snarled suddenly.

"Kid Wolf of Texas, sah," was the quiet reply.

A cold smile was on the sallow face of the don. He made no move to draw the jeweled revolver that hung at his hip. He sneered as he spoke:

"You will never escape from here alive, my friend," he leered. "What you have told me is not exactly news. At this moment you are covered."

"Yes?" mocked The Kid.

"Come in, major!" cried Don Floristo.

A door at one end of the room, which had been standing half ajar, now opened. Framed in the doorway was the bloated, fat figure of Major Stover. In his hand was a derringer. Its twin black muzzles were leveled at Kid Wolf's heart.

The major's face twisted into an exulting grin as his piglike eyes fell on Kid Wolf.

"We meet again," he grated.

"You see, Señor Keed Wolf," said Don Floristo, "that we have you. By accident, Señor Wolf, your plans miscarried. Thinking I could sell you a ranch, as you were buying cattle, I sent a rider *al instante* for my friend, the Major Stover. He came at once, and when I described you—" He laughed harshly.

The Don removed The Kid's revolvers and threw them on the table. The major's derringer did not waver.

"I see that yo' have prepared quite a surprise pahty fo' me," said The Kid calmly. "Remember that theah are all

142

sorts of surprises. I didn't have to come back heah, yo' know. The cattle I want are at Mariposa."

"Then why are you here, fool?" the don sneered.

"To find out who is at the bottom of the cattle stealin'—this persecution against Mrs. Thomas' ranch!" Kid Wolf snapped.

"What good is it to know?" asked Stover, laughing. "Yo're goin' to die!"

"Shoot him, major," said the don, baring his white teeth.

"There's no hurry," replied the major. "I want to see him pray for mercy first. I've got a score to settle with him."

The Kid remained unmoved in the presence of this peril. He was still smiling.

"Yuh'll never live to get those cattle across the line, blast yuh!" snarled Stover, trembling with rage. "It was a pretty little scheme, but it failed to work. And we've got the S Bar where we want it, too. No, yuh don't! Just keep yore hands over yore head."

"*El Lobo Muchacho,*" the don sneered. "*El Lobo Muchacho*—Keed Wolf. I think we have your fangs drawn now, Señor Wolf! The Wolf is in a bad way. Alas, he cannot bite." He finished with a cruel laugh.

But The Kid could bite—and did! One of the fangs of the wolf, and a deadly one, remained to him. He used it now!

Major Stover did not know how it happened. Kid Wolf's arms were lifted. Apparently he was helpless. But suddenly there was a swish—a lightning-like

143

gleam of light. Something hit Stover's gun arm like a thunder smash.

Kid Wolf had used his "ace in the hole"—had hurled the bowie knife hidden in a sheath sewn inside the back of his shirt collar.

The major's hand went suddenly numb. He dropped the derringer. The blade had thudded into his forearm and sliced deeply upward. Dazed, he emitted a wild cry.

The don was not slow to act. He did not know exactly what had happened, but he saw the major's gun fall and heard his frightened yell. Floristo reached hastily for his jewel-studded revolver.

But the Texan had closed in on him. Kid Wolf hit him full in the face and Floristo went sprawling down. He was still jerking at his gun butt as he hit the floor.

The major had recovered somewhat. With his left hand he scooped up the derringer and swung it up desperately to line the barrel on Kid Wolf's heart.

"All right, Harry!" sang out The Kid.

Glass flew out of the window at the south wall and clattered to the tiled floor as an arm, holding a leveled .45, broke through. It was young Thomas.

"Put 'em up!" he cried.

Don Floristo, however, had also raised his gun. A report shook the adobe walls and sent a puff of blue fumes ceilingward. But Harry Thomas had fired first. Floristo collapsed with a moan, rolled over and stiffened.

Kid Wolf sent Major Stover's derringer flying with a

contemptuous kick, just as the fear-crazed fat man pulled the trigger.

"Good work, Harry," The Kid approved.

He stepped to the table, returned his own six-guns to their holsters and then reached out and seized Major Stover by the collar. He shook him like a rat as he jerked him to his feet.

"Well, majah, as yo' calls yo'self," he drawled, "looks like the surprise worked the othah way round!"

Stover's flabby face was blue-gray. His knees gave way under him and his coarse lips were twitching. His eyes rolled wildly.

"Don't kill me," he wheezed in an agony of fright. "It wasn't my fault. I—I—Goliday made me do it. He's the man behind me. D-don't kill—me."

Suddenly his head rolled to one side and his bulky body wilted. He sagged to the floor with a hiccupping sound.

"Get up!" snapped the Texan.

There was no response. The Kid felt of Stover's heart and straightened up with a low whistle.

"Dead," he muttered. "Scared to death. Weak heart—just as I thought."

"Did yuh shoot the big brute?" asked Harry, who had pushed his body through the window and slipped into the room.

"His guilty conscience killed him," explained the Texan. "Yo' saved my life, son, by throwin' down on Don Floristo. Yo' got him between the shirt buttons."

"I wanted to shoot long before," said Harry, "but I

145

remembered—and waited until yuh said the word. Yuh shore stopped that derringer o' Stover's."

"Wheah's the guard?"

"Tied up outside."

"*Bueno.* I rode down heah slow, so yo'd have plenty o' time to get posted. I suspected treachery of some kind tonight. But it was a surprise to see the majah heah. What time is it?"

"After two. The moon's gone down. Where to, now?"

"To Mariposa. We can get theah by dawn, and if the boys are ready we can turn the trick."

"Then let's go, Kid!"

Five minutes later the two were pounding the trail northward toward the Rio Grande!

CHAPTER XV

GOLIDAY'S CHOICE

The east was streaked with pink and orange when The Kid and Harry Thomas rode into the sleeping town of Mariposa. The little Mexican city, they discovered, however, was not entirely asleep.

At the northern edge of the city, on the stretch of sand between the huddled adobes and the sandy waters of the Rio, things had taken place.

Harry and The Kid rode up to see a camp fire twinkling in the bottom of an arroyo just out of sight of Mariposa. Near it was the herd of six hundred steers, some down and resting, others milling restlessly about under the watchful eyes of three shadowy riders.

"Are those the don's men?" asked Harry in astonishment.

"Too far north," chuckled The Kid. "Look down by the fire!"

Tied securely with lariat rope, four figures reclined near the smoking embers. They were not Americans. The two grinning newcomers saw that, even before they made out their swarthy faces. The prisoners wore the dirty velvet jackets and big sombreros of Mexico.

"Theah's the don's men," said The Kid, laughing. "Come on!"

He rode toward one of the mounted shadows and whistled softly. The man turned. It was just light enough to make out his features. It was Anton.

"By golly, Kid," he yelped out. "Yo're here at last! We'd about give yuh up!"

"I see that yo' didn't wait fo' me," returned the Texan, smiling.

Wise and Lathum, seeing their visitors, spurred their mounts toward them. They greeted him with an exulting yell.

"We turned the trick!" Wise exclaimed. "Not a shot fired. Did it hours ago."

"Yuh see, Kid," said Anton, "we just naturally got so impatient and nervous waitin' that we couldn't stand it any longer. O' course, it was contrary to yore plans, maybe, but we saw the S Bar steers, stood it as long as we could, and swooped down. How yuh got 'em here and had 'em waitin' fer us like this is more'n I can see!"

"Yo' did well," approved Kid Wolf. "I thought maybe yo'd know what to do."

"Who is thet with yuh?" asked Anton, coming a bit closer. "Well, blamed if it ain't—Harry Thomas! Where—how—"

"Yes, it's me, boys," said Harry shamefacedly. "I've been a bad one, I know. But my friend, The Kid, here has opened my eyes to what's right. I want to go straight, and—" His voice trailed off.

"Harry's played the hand of a real man tonight," Kid Wolf put in for him.

"I'm through as a gambler," said Harry. "Boys, will yuh take me for a friend?"

"Well, I should say we will!" Lathum cried, and all three shook his hand warmly.

"Yore mother will be mighty proud, son—and glad," old Anton said.

"Now, men," said The Kid, "get those steers movin' toward the S Bar. Yuh ought to have 'em across the Rio by sunup. Theah won't be any pursuit. Don Floristo isn't in any position to ordah it. I'll see yo'-all at Ma Thomas' dinnah table."

"Where are you goin', Kid?" Lathum asked in astonishment.

"Harry will help yo' get the cattle home," said The Kid. "I'm ridin' like all get-out to make Mistah Goliday, Esquiah, a social call."

"But why—" Wise began.

"I've just remembahed," drawled The Kid, "wheah I

saw a pair of low-heeled, square-toed ridin' boots."

Anton gave a low whistle.

"By golly, boys. He's right! I remember now, too."

"So do I!" ejaculated Lathum.

"How about lettin' us go, too?" asked Wise. "Goliday has some hard hombres workin' for him, and—"

"Please leave this to me," begged The Kid. "Yo' duty is heah with these cattle. All mah life I've made it mah duty to right wrongs—and not only that, but to put the wrongdoers wheah they can't commit any mo' wrongs. Goliday is the mastah mind in all this trouble. Is theah a sho't cut to his ranch?"

Anton knew the trails of the district like a memorized map, and he gave The Kid detailed instructions. By following the mountain chain to the westward he would reach a dry wash that would lead him to a point within sight of Goliday's hacienda.

"Still set on it?"

The Kid nodded. "Adios! Yuh'll probably get through to the S Bar in good time. Good-by, Harry."

"Good luck!" they shouted after him.

At the crest of a mesquite-dotted swell of white sand, several hours later, The Kid paused to look over the situation that confronted him.

Ahead of him, to the westward, were the buildings of the Goliday ranch. Strangely enough, there was no sign of life around it—save for the horses in the large corral and the cattle meandering about the water hole.

Was the entire ranch personnel in San Felipe? Impossible! And yet he had seen no one. The Kid hoped that Goliday was not in town.

A desert wash led its twisting way to one side of him, and he saw that by following its course he could reach the trees about the water hole unobserved.

"Easy, Blizzahd," he said softly.

The sand deadened the sound of the big white horse's hoofs as it took the dry wash at a speedy clip. Kid Wolf crouched low, so that his body would not show above the edge of the wash. At the water hole he drew up in the shelter of a cottonwood to listen. His ears had caught a succession of steady, measured sounds. They came from one of the small adobe outbuildings. Inside, some one was hammering leather. This was the ranch's saddle shop evidently.

Very quietly The Kid dismounted. The saddle shop was not far away. He strolled toward it, wading through the sand that reached nearly to his ankles. He paused in the doorway, and the hammering sound suddenly ceased.

"Buenos dias," drawled the Texan.

The man in the shop was Goliday! He had whirled about like a cat. The hammer slipped from his right hand and dropped to the hard-packed earth floor with a thud.

Kid Wolf's eyes went from Goliday's dark, amazed face, with its shock of black hair, down to his boots. They were low-heeled, square-toed boots, embellished with scrolls done in red thread. The Kid's quiet glance traveled again back to Goliday's startled countenance.

150

Dismay and fury were mingled there. Kid Wolf had made no movement toward his guns. His hands were relaxed easily at his sides. He was smiling.

Goliday's ivory-handled gun was in his pistol holster. His hand moved a few inches toward it. Then it stopped. Goliday hesitated. Face to face with the show-down, he was afraid.

"Well," the ranchman's words came slowly, "what do yuh want with me?"

"I want yo'," said The Kid in a voice ringing like a sledge on solid steel, "fo' the murdah of the ownah of the S Bar!"

"Bah!" sneered Goliday, but a strange look crossed his dark eyes. His legs were trembling a little, either from excitement or nervousness.

"Yo're loco," he added. "My men are in town or I'd have yuh rode off of my place on a rail!"

"Goliday," snapped Kid Wolf crisply, "the man who shot Thomas down, wore low-heeled, square-toed boots."

"Yuh can't convict a man on that," replied the ranchman with a forced laugh.

"No?" The Kid drawled. "Well, that isn't all. The man who fired the death shot used a very peculiah revolvah—very peculiar. The caliber was .45. Wait a moment—a .45 with unusual riflin'."

"Yo're crazy," said Goliday, but his face was pale.

"By examinin' the cahtridge," continued the Texan in a dangerous voice, "I found that the fatal gun had five grooves and five lands. The usual six-shootah has six

151

grooves and six lands. Let me see yo' gun, sah!"

The command came like a whip-crack and little drops of perspiration stood out suddenly on Goliday's ashen forehead.

"It's a lie," he stammered. "I—"

"Yo' had bettah confess, Goliday. The game's up. Majah Stovah died early this mohnin' from heart trouble. Goliday, yo' can do just two things. The choice is up to yo'."

"The choice?" repeated the rancher mechanically.

"Yes, yo' can surrendah—and in that case, I'll turn yo' ovah to the nearest law, if it's a thousand miles away. Or—yo' can shoot it out with me heah and now. It's up to yo'."

"Yuh wanted to see my gun," said Goliday, with a sudden, deadly laugh. "All right, I'll show yuh what's in it!"

Like a flash his hairy right hand shot down toward the ivory-handled Colt.

The ranchman's hand touched the handle before Kid Wolf made even a move toward his own weapons. Goliday's eager, fear-accelerated fingers snapped the hammer back. The gun slid half out of its holster as he tipped it up.

There was a noise in the little adobe like a thunder-clap! A red pencil of flame streaked out between the two men. Then the smoke rolled out, dense and choking. *Thud! A* gun dropped to the hard, dirt floor.

Goliday groped out with his two empty hands for support. His face was distorted. A long gasp came from his lips. A round dot had suddenly appeared two inches left of his breast bone. He dropped heavily, grunting as he struck the ground.

Paying no more attention to him, Kid Wolf holstered his own smoking .45 and bent over and picked up Goliday's ivory-handled weapon. He smiled grimly as he peered into the muzzle. A very peculiar gun! There were five grooves and five lands, which are the spaces between the grooves, the uncut metal.

Goliday, with a bullet just below his heart, was not quite dead. He realized what had happened. He was done for. Rapidly, as if afraid that he could not finish what he wished to say, he began to speak:

"Yuh—were right. I killed Thomas. I wanted the S Bar. I'm afraid to go like this, Kid Wolf. I tell yuh I'm afraid!" His voice rose to a shriek. "There's murder on my soul, and there'll—be more. Quick! Quick!"

"Is there anything I can do?" The Kid asked, generous even to a fallen enemy such as Goliday.

"Yes," Goliday groaned. "All my men aren't in town. I sent Steve Stacy and Ed Mullhall—down to the S Bar—a little while ago—to do away with Mrs. Thomas. Stop 'em! Stop 'em! I don't want to die with this on my soul. I—I—"

His words ended in a gurgling moan. His face twitched and then relaxed. He was dead.

His dying words had thrilled Kid Wolf with horror. Steve Stacy and Ed Mullhall on their way to murder Ma Thomas! Perhaps they were at the S Bar already! Perhaps their terrible work was done! The Kid went white.

But he wasted no time in wringing his hands. At a dead run he left the saddle shop and the dead villain within it. He whistled for Blizzard. The horse raced to meet him. With a bound The Kid was in the saddle. He knew of no trail to the S Bar. He must cut across country. There was no time to hunt for one. Then, too, he must cut off as much as he could. In that way, if the two killers followed a more or less winding trail, he might overtake them.

The country was rough and broken. And, worse still, Blizzard was tired. He had been on the go for many hours. There was a limit even to the creamy-white horse's superb strength. It seemed hopeless. Southeast they tore at breakneck speed. Blizzard seemed to sense what was required of him. He ran like mad, clamping down on the bit, his muscles rippling under his glossy hide—a hide that was already flecked with foam.

"Go like yo' nevah went befo', Blizzahd boy," The Kid sobbed.

Never had he been up against a plot so ruthless, a situation more terrible. A lone woman, Ma Thomas, had been selected for the next victim!

As they pounded along, a thousand thoughts tortured the mind of The Kid. In a way, it was his fault. It was by his suggestion that Mrs. Thomas had returned to the ranch. Already, possibly, she was dead! Kid Wolf had never been angrier. The emotion that gripped him was more than anger. If he could only reach that S Bar in time!

He rode over hills of sand, across stretches of soft,

yielding sand that slowed even Blizzard's furiously drumming hoofs, over treacherous fields of lava rock, through cactus forests. Up and down he went, but always on, and always heading southward toward the ranch. Very rarely did The Kid use the spurs, but he used them now, roweling Blizzard desperately. And the white horse responded like a machine.

There is a limit to the endurance of any animal, however strong. Blizzard could not keep up that pace forever. He had begun to pant. He was running on sheer courage now. Then The Kid mounted a rise. Ahead of him he saw two moving dots—horsemen, bound toward the S Bar! They were Stacy and Mullhall, without a doubt!

Kid Wolf's heart leaped. They had not reached the ranch yet, at any rate. There was still hope. Again and again he raked Blizzard with the spurs. The horse was living up to his name now, running like a white snowstorm. Already the distance between Kid Wolf and the other horsemen was lessened. But they had seen him! Before, they had been riding at a leisurely pace. Now they broke into a gallop!

"Get 'em, Blizzahd," cried The Kid. "We've got to get those men, boy!"

Suddenly before The Kid a deep arroyo yawned. The walls were steep. There was no time to go around, or seek a place to make the crossing. It looked like the end. A full twenty feet! A tremendous leap, and for a tired horse—

"Jump it, boy! Jump it!"

Again Blizzard was raked with the spur. They were nearly at the arroyo edge now. It was very deep. Would Blizzard take it, or refuse?

Kid Wolf knew his horse. He already felt Blizzard rising madly in the air. The danger now was in the fall. For if the horse failed to make it, death would be the issue. Jagged rocks thirty feet below awaited horse and rider if the leap failed.

But Blizzard made it! He scrambled desperately on the far edge for a breathless moment while the soft sand caked and caved. The Kid threw his weight forward. Safely across, Blizzard was off again, galloping like a white demon.

Kid Wolf unlimbered one of his Colts. The range was almost impossible. Six times The Kid shot. One of the men toppled from his saddle and fell sprawling. The other rider kept on.

The Kid did not fire any more, for he knew that he had been lucky indeed, to get one of them at such a distance. He bent all his efforts toward heading off the other. Already the S Bar hacienda was within sight. There was no time to lose!

As The Kid pounded past he saw the face of the man who had been struck by the chance bullet. It was Mullhall. Stacy kept going. He was urging his horse to top speed, bent upon reaching the ranch and getting in his work before The Kid could catch him.

Blizzard had reached his limit. His pace was faltering. Little by little he began to lag behind. He was nearly spent. Only an expert rider could have done what The

Kid did then. Without slackening Blizzard's speed, he slipped his saddle. With the reins in his teeth, he worked loose the latigo and cinch, taking care not to trip the speeding horse. Then he swung himself backward, freed the saddle and blanket and hurled both sidewise. He was riding bareback now!

Relieved of forty pounds of dead weight, Blizzard lengthened his stride and took new courage. He was overhauling Stacy now yard by yard!

Stacy turned in his saddle and emptied his gun at his pursuer—six quick spats of smoke and six slugs of whining lead. All went wild, for it was difficult to aim at such a smashing gallop.

"We've got him now, boy," The Kid gasped. "Close in!"

Farther south, in the distance, he saw a great dust cloud moving in slowly. It was the riders with the recovered herd! But The Kid only had a glimpse. Steve Stacy was whirling about desperately to meet him. Once again The Kid was involved in a showdown to the bitter finish!

Kid Wolf's left-hand Colt sputtered from his hip. He had no more mercy for Stacy than he would have had for a rattlesnake that had bitten a friend.

Br-r-rang-bang! Spat-spat! Stacy, hit twice, still blazed away. A bullet ripped through the Texan's sleeve. Again he fired. The ex-foreman fell, part way. The stirrup caught his left foot as his head went into the sand. Stacy's horse reared back, started to run, then stopped and waited patiently for its master who would never rise.

　　　　　• • •

There was feasting at the S Bar hacienda. The table was heavily laden with dishes—once full of delicious viands but now empty. The men, five in all, had brought out their "makin's." Ma Thomas, bustling about with more coffee and a wonderful dessert she had mysteriously prepared, beamed down on them.

"You're surely not through already, are you, boys?" she protested. "Why, there's more pie and cake, and besides the—"

"I've et," sighed Anton, "until I'm about to bust."

There was a pause during which five matches were struck and applied to the ends of five cigarettes.

"Well," sighed Kid Wolf, "I hope Blizzahd has enjoyed his dinnah as much as I've enjoyed mine. He deserves it!"

"What a wonderful horse!" cried Ma Thomas. "And to think that if he hadn't ran so fast, those terrible men—" Her voice broke off.

"Now don't yo' worry of that any mo'," drawled The Kid with a smile. "Yo' troubles are ovah, I hope."

The Kid occupied the seat of honor, at Mrs. Thomas' right. Her son, Harry, as happy as he had ever been in his life, sat on the other. Anton, Wise, and Lathum were grouped about the rest of the table, leaning back in their chairs.

"When Blizzahd is rested," said The Kid, in a matter-of-fact tone, "we'll be strikin' westward. I'm kind of anxious to see what's doin' ovah in New Mexico and Arizona."

"Yo're surely not goin' to leave us so soon!" they all cried.

The Kid nodded.

"Mah work seems to be done heah," he said, smiling. "And I'm just naturally a rollin' stone, always rollin' toward new adventures. I'm sho' yo'-all are goin' to be very happy."

"We owe it all to you!" Ma Thomas cried. "All of our good fortune. I have the ranch and the cattle, and more wonderful than everything else—my boy, Harry!"

Kid Wolf looked embarrassed. "Please don't try and thank me," he murmured. "It's just mah job—to keep an eye out fo' those in need of help."

"Won't yuh take a half interest in the S Bar, Kid?" Harry begged.

Kid Wolf shook his head.

"But, say," blurted Harry. He leaned across the table to whisper:

"How about all that money in that poker game down in Mariposa? It's yores, not mine!"

"I did that," said The Kid, as he whispered back, "so yo' could buy Ma a little present. Don't forget! A nice one!"

"What did I ever—ever do to deserve this happiness?" Ma Thomas sighed, and she interrupted the furtive conversation of the two young men by placing a big dish of shortcake between them.

"By gettin' aftah me with a shotgun," said Kid Wolf with a laugh.

CHAPTER XVI

A GAME OF POKER

A whitened human skull, fastened to a post by a rusty tenpenny nail, served as a signboard and notified the passing traveler that he was about to enter the limits of Skull, New Mexico.

"Oh, we're ridin' 'way from Texas, and the Rio,
  Comin' to a town with a mighty scary name,
Shall we turn and vamos pronto for the Rio,
Or show some hombres how to make a wild
  town tame?"

Kid Wolf, who appeared to be asking Blizzard the rather poetical question, eyed the gruesome monument with a half smile. Bullet holes marked it here and there, testifying that many a passer-by with more marksmanship than respect had used it for a casual target. The empty sockets seemed to glare spitefully, and the shattered upper jaw grinned in mockery at the singer. It was as if the grisly relic had heard the song and laughed. Kid Wolf's smile flashed white against the copper of his face. Then his smile disappeared and his eyes, blue-gray, took on frosty little glints.

The Kid, after straightening out the troubled affairs of the Thomas family, was heading northwest again. It was the age-old wanderlust that led him out of the

Rio country once more.

"What do yo' say, Blizzahd?" he drawled.

His tones held just a trace of sarcasm. It was as if he had weighed the veiled threat in the town's sign and found it grimly humorous instead of sinister.

The big white horse threw up its shapely head in a gesture of impatience that was almost human.

"All right, Blizzahd," approved its rider. "Into Skull, New Mexico, we go!"

Kid Wolf had heard something of Skull's reputation, and although it was just accident that had turned him this way, he was filled with a mild curiosity. The Texan never made trouble, but he was hardly the man to avoid it if it crossed his path.

As he neared the town, he was rather surprised at its size. The budding cattle industry had boomed the surrounding country, and Skull had grown like a mushroom. Lights were twinkling in the twilight from a hundred windows, and as the newcomer passed the scattered adobes at the edge of it, he could hear the *clip-clop* of many horses, the sound of men's voices, and mingled strains of music. The little city was evidently very much alive.

There were two principal streets, cutting each other at right angles, each more than a hundred yards long and jammed with buildings of frame and sod. Kid Wolf read the signs on them as the horse trotted southward:

"Bar. Tony's Place. Saloon. General merchandise. Saddle shop. Bar. Saloon. Hotel and bar. Well, well, seems as if we have mo' than ouah share o' saloons

161

heah. This seems to be the biggest one. Shall we stop heah, Blizzahd?"

There seemed to be no choice in the matter. One could take his pick of saloons, for nothing else was open at this hour. The sign over the largest read, "The Longhorn Palace."

Kid Wolf left Blizzard at the hitch rack and sauntered through the open doors. A lively scene met his eyes. It interested and at the same time disgusted The Kid. A long bar stretched from the front door to the end of the building, and a dozen or more men leaned against it in various stages of intoxication. In spite of the fact that the saloon interior was well lighted by suspended oil lamps, the air was thick and foul with liquor fumes and cigarette smoke. A half dozen gambling tables, all busy, stood at the far end of the room.

The mirror behind the bar was chipped here and there with bullet marks, and over it were three enormous steer heads with wide-spreading horns. It was evident that drunken marksmen had taken pot shots at these ornaments, also, for they were pitted here and there with .45 holes. Kid Wolf was by no means impressed. He had been in bad towns aplenty, and he usually found that the evil of them was pure bluff and bravado. Smiling, he strolled over to the gambling tables.

The stud-poker table attracted his attention, first by the size of the stakes and then by the men gathered there. It was a stiff game, opening bets sometimes being as much as fifty dollars. Apparently the lid was off.

The hangers-on in the Longhorn seemed to be of one

type and resembled professional gunmen more than they did cattlemen. The men at the poker table looked like desperadoes, and one of them especially took The Kid's observing eye.

A huge-chested man in a checkered shirt was at the head of the table and seemed to have the game well in hand, for his chip stacks were high, and a pile of gold pieces lay behind them. His closely cropped black beard could not conceal the cruelty of his flaring nostrils and sensual mouth. He was overbearing and loud of speech, and his menacing, insolent stare seemed to have every one cowed.

Kid Wolf was a keen student of men. He had learned to read human nature, and this gambler interested him as a thoroughly brutal specimen.

"It'll cost yuh-all another hundred to stay and see this out," the bearded man announced with a sneer.

"I'm out," grunted one of the players.

Another, with "more in sight" than the bearded gambler, turned over his cards in disgust, and with a chuckle of joy, the first speaker dragged in the pot and added the chips to his mounting stacks. He seemed to have the others buffaloed.

The card players had been absorbed in their game until now. But as the new deal was begun, the bearded gambler saw the Texan's eyes upon him.

"Are yuh starin' at me?" he rasped. "Walk away, or get in—one o' the two. Yuh'll kill my luck."

"Pahdon me, sah. I don't think I could kill such luck as yo's."

The Kid's voice was full of soothing politeness. The gambler made the mistake of thinking the stranger in awe of him. Many a man before him had taken the Texan's soft, drawling speech the wrong way.

"Well, are yuh gettin' in the game?"

"I'm not a gamblin' man, sah." The Texan smiled.

The bearded man exposed his teeth in a contemptuous leer.

"From yore talk, yo're nothin' but a cheap cotton picker. Guess this game's too stiff fer yuh," he said.

The expression of the Texan's face did not change, but curious little flecks of light appeared in his steel-like eyes. He laughed quietly.

"I'd get in," he said, "but I'd hate to take yo' money."

"Don't let that worry yuh," the big-chested gambler snarled. "Sit in, or shut up and get out!"

If Kid Wolf was angered, he made no sign of it. His lips still smiled, as he drew a chair up to the table.

"Deal me in," he drawled.

The atmosphere of the game seemed to change. It was as if all the players had united to fleece the newcomer, with the bearded desperado leading the attack.

At first, Kid Wolf lost, and the gambler—called "Blacksnake" McCoy by the other men—added to his chip stacks. Then the game seesawed, after which the Texan began to win small bets steadily. But the crisis was coming. Sooner or later, Blacksnake would try to run Kid Wolf out, and the Texan knew it.

The size of the bets increased, and a little crowd began to gather about the stud table. In spite of the fact that Blacksnake was a swaggering, abusive-mouthed fellow, the sympathies of the Longhorn loafers seemed to be with him.

He seemed to be a sort of leader among them, and a group of sullen-eyed gunmen were looking on, expecting to see Kid Wolf beaten in short order.

Finally a tenseness in the very air testified to the fact that the time for big action had come. The pot was already large, and all had dropped out except Black-snake and the drawling stranger.

"I'm raisin' yuh five hundred, 'Cotton-picker,'" sneered the bearded man insolently.

He had a pair of aces in sight—a formidable hand—and if his hole card was also an ace, Kid Wolf had not a chance in the world. The best the Texan could show up was a pair of treys.

"My name, sah," said Kid Wolf politely, "is not Cotton-pickah, although that is bettah than 'Bone-pickah'—an appropriate name fo' some people. I'm Kid Wolf, sah, from Texas. And my enemies usually learn to call me by mah last name. I'm seein' yo' bet and raisin' yo' another five hundred, sah."

At the name "Kid Wolf," a stir was felt in the crowded saloon. It was a name many of them had heard before, and most of the loungers began to look upon the stranger with more respect. Others frowned darkly. Blacksnake was one of them. Plainly, what he had heard of The Kid did not tend to make the latter popular in his estimation.

"Excuse me," he spat out. "I should have called yuh

165

'Nose-sticker.' From what I hear of yuh, yuh have a habit of mindin' other folks' business. Well, that ain't healthy in Skull."

If the Texan was provoked by these insults, he did not show it. He only smiled gently.

"We're playin' pokah now, I believe," he reminded. "Are yuh seein' mah bet?"

"That's right, bet 'em like yuh had 'em. And I hope yore hole card's another three-spot, for that'll make it easy for my buried ace. I'm seein' yuh and boostin' it— for yore pile!"

Quietly The Kid swept all his chips into the center of the table. He had called, and it was a show-down.

With an oath, Blacksnake got half to his feet. He turned his hole card over. It was a nine-spot, but he had Kid Wolf beaten unless—

Slowly The Kid revealed his hole card. It was not a trey, but a four. Just as good, for this made him two small pairs—threes and fours. He had won!

"No," he drawled, "I wouldn't reach for my gun, if I were yo'."

Blacksnake took his hand away from the butt of his .45. It came away faster than it had gone for it. Guns had appeared suddenly in the Texan's two hands. His draw had been so swift that nobody had caught the elusive movement.

"This game is bein' played with cahds, even if they are crooked cahds, and not guns, sah!"

"Crooked!" breathed Blacksnake. "Are yuh hintin' that I'm a crook?"

"I'm not hintin'," said The Kid, with a flashing smile. "I'm sayin' it right out. The aces in that deck were marked in the cornahs with thumbnail scratches. It might have gone hahd with me, if I hadn't mahked the othah cahds too—with thumbnail scratches!"

"Yuh admit yuh marked them cards?" yelled Blacksnake in fury. "What about it, men? He's a cheat and ought to be strung up!"

Most of the onlookers were doing their best to conceal grins, and even Blacksnake's sympathizers made no move to do anything. Perhaps The Kid's two drawn six-shooters had something to do with it.

"Yuh got two thousand dollars from this game—twenty hundred even," Blacksnake snarled. "Are yuh goin' to return that money?"

"I'll put the money wheah it belongs," the Texan drawled. "Gentlemen, when I said I wasn't a gamblin' man, I meant it. I nevah gamble. But when I saw that this game was not a gamble, but just a cool robbery, I sat in."

He holstered one of his guns and swooped up the pile of money from the center of the table. This cleaned it, save for one pile of chips in front of the bearded bully.

"It's customary," said Kid Wolf, "always to kick in with a chip fo' the 'kitty,' and so—"

His Colt suddenly blazed. There was a quick finger of orange-colored fire and a puff of smoke. The top chip of Blacksnake's stack suddenly had disappeared, neatly clipped off by The Kid's bullet. And the Texan had shot casually from the hip, apparently without taking aim!

Kid Wolf returned his still-smoking gun to its holster, turned his back and sauntered leisurely toward the door. Halfway to it, he turned quickly. He did not draw his guns again, but only looked Blacksnake steadily in the eyes.

"Remembah," he said, "that I can see yo' in the mirrah."

With an oath, Blacksnake took his hand away from his gun butt, toward which it had been furtively traveling. He had forgotten about the bullet-scarred glass over the long bar.

As the Texan strolled through the door, a man who had been watching the scene turned to follow him.

"Kid Wolf," he called, "I'd like to see yuh, alone."

The voice was friendly. Kid Wolf turned, and as he did so, he jostled the speaker, apparently by accident.

"Excuse me," drawled the Texan. "I didn't know yo' were so close behind me."

"I'm a friend," said the other earnestly. "Let's walk down the street a way. I've something important to say—something that might interest yuh."

The Kid had appraised him at a glance, although this stranger was far from being an ordinary person either in face or dress. His garb was severe and clerical. He wore a long black coat, black trousers neatly tucked into boots, a white shirt, and a flowing dark tie. Yet he was not of the gambler type. He seemed to be unarmed, for he had no gun belt. His face, seen from the reflected lights of the saloon, was clean-shaven. His eyes seemed set too close together, and the lips were very thin.

"Very well, I'll listen," The Kid consented.

The two started to walk slowly down the board side-walk.

"They call me 'Gentleman John,'" said the black-clothed stranger. "Have yuh been in Skull long? Expect to stay hereabouts for a while?"

The Texan answered both these questions shortly but politely. He had arrived that evening, he said, and he wasn't sure how long he would remain in the vicinity.

"How would yuh like," tempted the man who had styled himself Gentleman John, "to make a hundred dollars a day?"

"Honestly?" asked The Kid.

The man in black pursed his lips and spread out his palms significantly.

"Whoever heard of a gunman making that much honestly?" he laughed coldly. "Maybe I should tell yuh somethin' about myself. They call me the 'Cattle King of New Mexico.' The man yuh bucked in the poker game—Blacksnake McCoy—is at the head of my—ah—outfit."

"Oh," said The Kid softly, "yo're that kind of a cattle king."

"Out here," Gentleman John leered, "the Colt is power. I've got ranches, cattle. I've managed to do well. I need gunmen—men who can shoot fast and obey orders. I can see that yo're a better man than Blacksnake. I'm payin' him fifty a day. Take his job, and yuh'll get a hundred."

Kid Wolf did not seem in the least enthusiastic, and the man in black went on eagerly:

"Yuh won a couple o' thousand tonight, Kid. But that won't last forever. Think what a hundred in gold a day means. And all yuh have to do is ter—"

"Murdah!" snapped the Texan. "Yo've mistaken yo' man, sah. Mah answah is 'no'! I'm not a hired killah, and the man who tries to hire me had bettah beware. Why, yo're nothin' but a cheap cutthroat!"

The cold eyes of the other suddenly blazed. He made a quick motion toward his waistcoat with his thin hand.

Kid Wolf laughed quietly. "Heah's yo' gun, sah," he said, handing the astonished Gentleman John a small, ugly derringer. "When I bumped into yo' in the doorway, I took the liberty to remove it. I nevah trust an hombre with eyes like yo's. Nevah mind tryin' to use it, fo' I've unloaded it."

The face of the man in black was white with fury. His gimlet eyes had narrowed to slits, and his mouth was distorted with rage. It was the face of a killer—a murderer without conscience or pity.

"I'll get yuh for this, Wolf!" he bellowed. "Yuh'll find out how strong I am here. This country isn't big enough to hold us both, blast yuh! When our trails meet again, take care!"

The Kid raised one eyebrow. "I always do take care," he drawled. "And while I'm heah in Skull County, yo'd bettah keep yo' dirty work undah covah. Adios!"

And humming musically under his breath, The Kid strolled toward the hitch rack where he had left his horse.

CHAPTER XVII

POT SHOTS

There was an old mission at the outskirts of the town of Skull, established many years before there were any other buildings in the vicinity. The Spanish fathers had built it for the Indians, and it remained a sanctuary, in spite of the roughness and badness of the new cow town.

Early on the morning after Kid Wolf's arrival in the town, the old padre was astonished to find a package of money inside his door. It was addressed simply: "For the poor." It was a windfall and a much-needed addition to the mission's meager finances.

The padre considered it a gift from Heaven, and where it had come from remained a mystery. The package contained two thousand dollars. Needless to say, it was Kid Wolf's gift, and the money had been taken from the town's dishonest gamblers.

The Texan remained several days in Skull. He was in no hurry, and the town interested him. Although he heard threats, he was left alone. He saw no more of Gentleman John, nor did he see Blacksnake McCoy. They had disappeared from town, probably on evil business of their own.

A note thrust under The Kid's door at the hotel two mornings later threatened him and advised him to leave the country. The Texan, however, paid no attention to the warning.

The next day, he scouted about the country, sizing up the cattle situation. The honest cattlemen, he found, were very much in the minority. By force, murder, and illegal methods, Gentleman John had obtained most of the land and practically all of the vast cattle herds that roamed the rich rangelands surrounding the town on all sides. Yet to most of the honest element, Gentleman John's true colors were not known. He shielded himself, hiring others to do his unclean work. There was no law as yet in the county. Gentleman John had managed to keep it out. And even if there had been, it was doubtful if his crimes could be pinned to him, for he had covered his tracks well. Many thought him honest. Only The Kid's keen mind could sense almost immediately what was going on.

The country stretching out from Skull was wild and beautiful. It was an unsettled land, and the trails that led into it were faint and difficult to follow.

One morning, Kid Wolf saddled Blizzard and rode into the southwest toward the purple mountains tipped with snow. It was a beautiful day, cool and crisp. The tang of the air in that high altitude was sharp and invigorating. The big white horse swung into a joyous lope, and the Texan hummed a Southern melody.

Crossing a wide stretch of plain, they mounted a rise,

and the character of the country changed. The smell of sage gave way to the penetrating odor of small pine, as they climbed into the broken foothills that led, in a series of steps, toward the jagged peaks. Splashing through a little creek of pure, cold water, The Kid turned Blizzard's head up a pass between two ridges of piñon-covered buttes.

"A big herd's passed this way," The Kid muttered, "and lately, too."

They climbed steadily onward, while the Texan searched the trail with keen eyes that missed nothing. Suddenly he drew up his horse. Blizzard had shied at something lying prone ahead of them, and The Kid's eyes had seen it at the same instant.

Stretched out on the sandy ground, The Kid saw, when he urged his horse closer, was the body of a man, face down and arms flung out. A blotch of red on the blue of the shirt told the significant story—a bullet had got in its deadly work. Dismounting, the Texan found that the man was dead and had met with his wound probably twenty-four hours before. There was nothing with which to identify the body.

"Seems to me, Blizzahd," Kid Wolf mused, "that Gentleman John is a deepah-dyed villain than we even thought."

He continued on up the pass, eyes and ears open. The white horse took the climb as if it had been level ground, his hoofs ringing a brisk tattoo against the stones.

Nobody was in sight. The land stretched out on all

173

sides—a vast lonesomeness of rolling green and red, broken here and there by towering rocks, grotesque in shape and twisted by erosion into a thousand fanciful sculptures. But at the bottom of a dry wash, Kid Wolf received a surprise.

Br-r-reee! Ping! A bullet breezed by his head, droning like a hornet, and glanced sullenly against a flat rock. Immediately afterward, The Kid heard the sharp bark of a .45. He knew by the sound of the bullet and by the elapsed time between it and the sound of the gun that he was within dangerous range. Crouching low in his saddle, he wheeled Blizzard—already turned half around in mid-air—and cut up the arroyo at a hot gallop.

Flinging himself from his horse when he reached shelter, he touched Blizzard lightly on the neck. The wise animal knew what that meant. Without slackening its pace, it continued onward, its hoofs drumming a rapid *clip-clop,* while its master was running in another direction with his head low.

Breaking up the ambush was easy. The Kid took advantage of every bit of cover and went directly toward the sounds of the shots, for guns were still barking. The men, whoever they were, were shooting in the direction of the riderless horse. Squirming through a little piñon thicket, Kid Wolf saw three men stationed behind a low ledge of red sandstone. The guns of the trio were still curling blue smoke.

"Will yo' kindly stick up yo' hands, gentlemen," the Texan drawled, "while yo're explainin'?"

The three whirled about—to find themselves staring into the two deadly black muzzles of The Kid's twin six-shooters. Automatically they thrust their arms aloft.

"Well, I guess yuh got us! Go ahead and shoot, yuh killer!"

Kid Wolf looked at the speaker in surprise. He was a little younger, perhaps, than the Texan himself—a slim, red-headed youth with a wide, determined mouth. The blue eyes, snapping angrily now, seemed frank and open. Then the Texan's eyes traveled to the youth's two companions. Both were older men, typical cowpunchers, rough and ready, and yet hardly of the same type of the men The Kid had noticed in the Longhorn Saloon in Skull.

"I'm not sure that I even want to shoot." The Kid smiled slowly. "Maybe yo'd like to explain why yo' were tryin' to shoot me."

"I guess we won't need to explain that," snapped the redhead. "Yuh know as well as we do that yo're one o' Blacksnake's thievin' gunmen!"

"What makes yo' think so?" the Texan laughed.

The other opened his mouth to speak, then stopped. He was looking The Kid up and down.

"Come to think about it," he muttered, "we've never seen you before. And yuh don't look like one o' that rustler gang."

"Take my word fo' it," said the Texan earnestly, "I'm not. I thought yo' were Blacksnake and his gang myself." He reholstered his guns. "Put yo' hands

175

down," he said, as he came toward them, "and we'll talk this thing ovah."

Reassured, the trio did so with sighs of relief. A few questions by each helped to clear things up. The Kid told them who he was, and in return he was told that the three were members of the Diamond D outfit.

"It's just half an outfit now," said the red-haired youth bitterly. "They've run off our north herd. Yuh see, Mr. Wolf—"

"Just call me 'Kid,'" smiled the Texan, "fo' I think we'll be friends."

"I hope so," said the other, flashing him a grateful look. "Well, I'm 'Red' Morton. My brother and me own the Diamond D, and we've shore been havin' one hot time. Guess we're plumb beat."

"Wheah's yo' brother now?"

"He's at the sod house with our south herd. These two men are the only punchers left me—'Lefty' Warren and Mike Train. There was one more. The rustlers shot him." Red Morton's eyes gleamed fiercely.

"Yo' know who the rustlers were?"

"Blacksnake McCoy's gang. He's been causin' us a lot o' trouble. Until now, that bunch have just been runnin' a smooth iron and swingin' their loops wide. But yesterday they drove off every steer. Half of all the longhorns on the Diamond D!" Red's lips tightened grimly.

"Excuse us," spoke up one of the cowboys, Lefty Warren, "for takin' yuh fer one o' them cutthroats, but we was b'ilin' mad. It's a good thing fer us yuh wasn't.

176

Yuh shore slipped in on us slick as a whistle."

"I'm hopin' my bud, Joe, don't think it was my fault that Blacksnake got away with the herd," groaned the red-haired youth. "Reckon we'll have to sell out now."

"That's it," agreed the eldest of the trio—the man called Mike Train. "The Diamond D would be on Easy Street now, if we had the cattle back. The mortgage—"

"Who would yo' sell to?" asked The Kid quietly.

"Gentleman John, the cattle king," explained Red Morton. "He told my brother some time ago that he'd like to buy it, if the price was low. Joe refused then, but reckon it'll be different now."

Kid Wolf raised his brows slightly.

"Is this—ah—Gentleman John the right sort of hombre?" he drawled.

"Why, I guess so," said Red in surprise. "He's one o' the biggest cattlemen in three States."

The Texan was silent for a moment, then he smiled.

"Wheah are yo' headed fo' now?" he asked.

"Why, we're on the trail of the stolen herd," Red replied, "and we intend to stop at the sod house and tell my brother, Joe, what's happened—that is, if he don't already know. Maybe he's had trouble, himself."

"If we find any of that Blacksnake gang, we'll fight," Lefty Warren spoke up. "The odds are mighty bad against us, but they got one o' the best punchers in the valley when they drilled Sam Whiteman."

"I'm interested," Kid Wolf told them. "Do yo' mind if I throw in with yo'?"

177

"Do we mind?" repeated Red joyously. "Say, it would shore be great! And—well, Joe and I will try and make it right with yuh."

"Nevah mind that," the Texan murmured. "Just considah yo' troubles mine, too. And I'm downright curious to know what's happened to yo' steers. Let's go!" He whistled for Blizzard.

For several hours the quartet of horsemen pressed southward, following the trail left by the stolen beef herd. The four quickly became friends. Kid Wolf liked them all from the first, and the Diamond D men were overjoyed to have him enlisted in their cause. He learned that Red Morton and his older brother, Joe, had worked hard to make the Diamond D a success. The ranch had been left them by their father a few years before, heavily burdened with debt. Now, until the catastrophe of the day before, they were at the point of clearing it. Evidently the brothers did not know of Gentleman John's criminal methods, and the Texan said nothing. He was waiting for better proof.

"The ranch is in Joe's name," said Red proudly, "but we're partners. He could sell it to Gentleman John, all right, without my consent, but he wouldn't. I'm not quite twenty-one, but I'm a man, and Joe knows it."

"Will yo' have to sell the Diamond D now?" the Texan asked.

"I hope not. Joe and two riders still have the south herd—at least, they have if nothin's happened. It might pull us through. Eight hundred head."

After a time, they swung off the trail they had been

following, in order to reach the sod house. Here Red expected to find his brother and the other two Diamond D riders.

"With them, that'll make seven of us," young Morton said. "Then we can show that Blacksnake gang a fight that is a fight! There's over a dozen of 'em, though I think Lefty here wounded one, just after Whiteman was killed. We saw red stains on the sagebrush for a hundred yards along the cattle trail."

Mounting a long rise, they began to descend again. A fertile valley stretched out beneath them, green with grass and watered by the bluest little stream that Kid Wolf had ever seen. It was a lovely spot; it was small wonder that Gentleman John wished to add the Diamond D to his holdings.

"That's Blue-bottle Creek," announced Red Morton. "Queer that we don't see any cattle. There's not a steer in sight. They ought to be feedin' through here."

There was no sign of anything moving throughout all the basin, either human or cattle. The silence was unbroken, save for the steady drumming of the little party's pony hoofs.

"There's the sod house—over there in those trees," said Red, after another mile.

He was worried. The two other Diamond D men, too, were showing signs of nervousness. Had the south herd gone the way of the other?

They neared the sod house—a structure crudely built of layers of earth. It had one door and one window, and near it was a corral—empty. There was

179

no sign of any one about, and there was no reply to Red's eager shout.

"Oh, Joe!" he hailed.

His face was a shade paler, as he quickly swung himself out of his saddle. He entered the sod house at a half run.

"Is anything wrong?" Train shouted.

Then they heard Red Morton cry out in grief and horror. Without waiting for anything more, The Kid and the two Diamond D riders dismounted and raced toward the sod hut. None of them was prepared for the terrible thing they found there.

CHAPTER XVIII

ON BLACKSNAKE'S TRAIL

At first, they could see little, for not much light filtered through the small door and window. Then details of the interior began to grow more distinct in the hut's one room. A tarp had been tacked over the dirt ceiling to keep scorpions and centipedes from dropping down on the bunks below. There was only a little furniture, and that of a crude sort. Some of it was smashed, as if in a scuffle.

These things, however, were not noticed until later. What the visitors saw was the form of a man with legs and arms outstretched at queer angles.

Kid Wolf was accustomed to horrible sights, but he

remembered this one ever afterward. The scene was stamped on his mind like a fragment of some wild nightmare.

The body was that of a man a few years older than Red Morton, and the features, though set and twisted, were the same. A rope had been tied to one wrist and fastened to one wall; another rope had been knotted about his other wrist and secured to the opposite side of the hut. The legs had been served the same way at the ankles. On the body of the suspended figure rocks had been piled. They were of many sizes, varying from a few pounds to several hundred. It was easy to see how the unhappy man had met his end—by slow torture. One by one, the rocks had been placed on his chest and middle, the combined weight of them first slowly pulling his limbs from their sockets and then crushing out the life that remained.

Red, after his first outcry of agony, took it bravely. The Kid threw his arm sympathetically around the youth's shoulders and drew him away, while the others cut the ropes that held the victim of the rustler gang's cruelty. In a few minutes, Red got a grip on himself and could talk in a steady voice.

"Reckon I'm alone now, Kid," he blurted. "Joe was all I had—and they got him! I swear I'll bring those hounds to justice, or die a-tryin'!"

"Yo're not alone, Red," said the Texan grimly. "I'm takin' a hand in this game."

Near the body they found a piece of paper—a significant document, for it explained the motive for the crime. Kid Wolf read it and understood. It was written in straggling handwriting:

I, Joe Morton, do hereby sell and turn over all interest in the Diamond D Ranch property, for value received. My signature is below, and testifies that I have sold said ranch to Gentleman John, of Skull, New Mexico.

There was, however, no signature at the space left at the bottom of the paper. Joe Morton had died game!

"He refused to sign," said The Kid quietly, "and that means that yo're the lawful heir to the Diamond D. Yo' have a man's job to do now, Red."

"But I don't savvy this," burst out the red-haired youth. "Surely this Gentleman John isn't—"

"He's the man behind it all, mah boy," the Texan told him. And in a few words, he related how he had been approached by the self-styled cattle king, and something of his shady dealings. "He wanted to buy me," he concluded, "not knowin' that I had nevah abused the powah of the Colt fo' mah own gain. Blacksnake is his chief gunman, actin' by Gentleman John's ordahs."

"Where's the other men—the two riders on duty with Joe?" Lefty Warren wanted to know.

It did not take much of a search to find them. One had fallen near the little corral, shot through the heart. The other lay a few hundred yards away, at the river bank. He, too, was dead.

"Mo' murdah," snapped the Texan grimly. "Well, we must make ouah plans."

In this sudden crisis, the other three left most of the planning to Kid Wolf himself. First of all, the bodies were buried. Rocks were piled on the hastily made graves to keep the coyotes out, and they were ready to go again.

The Texan decided to follow the trails left by the stolen cattle, for both herds were gone now, driven off the Diamond D range. Failing in their attempt to get Joe Morton's signature, the outlaws had evidently decided to take what they could get.

There was one big reason why Gentleman John wished to get his hands on the Diamond D. Although land was plentiful in that early day, Red's father had obtained a land grant from a Spanish governor—a grant that still held good and kept other herds from the rich grazing land and ample water along Blue-bottle Creek.

As they started down the trail again toward the broken, mountainous country to the southwest, The Kid sent Red a quick glance.

"Are yo' all right, son?" he asked.

"Fine," said young Morton, now sole owner of the Diamond D.

The Texan was glad to see that he had braced himself. Like his brother, Red was a man.

"We'll soon overtake 'em," old Mike Train muttered, savagely twirling the cylinder of his ancient .45. "Blacksnake's gang can't make fast time with those steers. He's probably drivin' 'em to Gentleman John's headquarters at Agua Frio."

"Why," asked Kid Wolf slowly, "do they call that hombre 'Blacksnake'?"

"Because he carries one with him—that's how he got his name," spoke up Lefty Warren. "He's a whipper. He's beaten more'n one Mex to death with it, and they say a white man or two. He can handle a blacksnake like a demon."

Kid Wolf smiled grimly. To have Blacksnake McCoy for an enemy was by no means a pleasant thing to think about, especially when the desperado was backed by all the power that his employer—Gentleman John—possessed. And yet The Kid was afraid of neither of them.

"It's shore great of yuh to help us this way," Red told him. "But I'm afraid we haven't a chance. If Gentleman John is behind all this, we're buckin' mighty big odds."

"I like a game like that," said The Kid. "Unlike pokah, it's perfectly legitimate to scratch the aces with yo' fingah nail."

They were soon off the limits of the Diamond D and on the Casas Amarillas—a ranch owned by Gentleman John and taking its Spanish name from two yellow houses of adobe several miles distant. They saw scattered cattle branded with a Lazy J—one of Gentleman John's many brands—but discovered no stragglers from the stolen Morton herds.

Following the trail was easy, and they struck a hot pace down through and out of the grassy valley, climbing through a pass and up on a rolling mesa dotted

184

with thirsty-looking sage. For two full hours they rode, while the sun crept toward the west. Their horses were beginning to tire. A line of cedar-sprinkled hills loomed up ahead of them, but by keeping to the plateau they could circle them.

"I think we'd bettah keep to the mesa," The Kid advised.

"But we're about on 'em," put in Red. "They'll see us comin', miles away. If we cut down through those hills, we'll gain time, too, and keep hid."

"It's a fine place to be trapped in," mused the Texan. "Well, Red, yo' know this country, an' I don't, so use yo' own judgment."

Against the far horizon they could make out a faint yellow haze—dust from the trampling hoofs of many cattle. They could cut off a full mile by riding down into the cedars, and Red decided to do so. The Kid was dubious, but said nothing more. If Blacksnake had a rear guard of any kind, they might have been sighted. In that case, they would run into trouble—ambushed trouble.

Kid Wolf rode in the lead, the three others drumming along behind him. He was grimly wary. A chill gust of wind hit them, as they entered the depths of the notch between the hills. The straggling growth of cedars and stumpy evergreens loomed up ahead of them, and they crashed through. For several hundred yards they tore their way and found their pace slowed by the difficult going. The trees began to thin out. Then they heard a spring tinkling down among the red rocks, and the cedars began to thicken again, as the little canyon narrowed and climbed steeply.

"Stick 'em up!"

Kid Wolf fired at the sound of the voice while the loud shout was still echoing. His double draw was lightning fast. Before the others knew what was taking place, his two guns had flashed. At the dull boom of the twin explosions, a crashing sound was heard in the brush, as if something was wildly threshing about. Then bullets began to rip and smash their way through the undergrowth. Cedar twigs flew.

With a yell, Mike Train slumped down over his saddle pommel and rolled off his horse. At the same instant, the two others—Lefty Warren and Red Morton—reached for their guns. The thing had happened so quickly that until now they had not thought of drawing their weapons.

But Kid Wolf stopped them.

"Don't pull 'em, boys!" he cried. And at the same time, he dropped both his own guns. It was a surprising thing for the Texan to do, but his mind had worked quickly. His sharp eyes had taken in the situation. They were covered, and from all sides. His first quick shots had brought one man down, but there were at least six others, and all were behind shelter and had a deadly drop. If The Kid had been alone, he would, no doubt, have shot it out there and then, using his own peculiar tactics. But he had the others to think of. If they touched their guns, they would be killed instantly.

The Texan's doubts had been well founded. They

should have kept to the mesa top. They had jumped into a trap. Surrender was the only thing to do now, for while there was life, there was hope. The Kid had slipped from tight situations before.

Lefty Warren, Red Morton, and The Kid elevated their hands. A low laugh came from behind the cedar thicket, and a group of desperadoes on foot slipped through, holding drawn and leveled Colts. In the lead was Blacksnake McCoy. His eyes fell on Kid Wolf and widened with surprise. Then his teeth showed through his close-cropped beard in a snarl of hate.

"Well, if it ain't the gamblin' Cotton-picker!" he ejaculated. "I didn't know I was goin' to have such luck as this! Keep yore mitts up, the three of yuh. Pedro, collect their guns!"

A grinning desperado disarmed Lefty and Red and picked up The Kid's two Colts.

"It'd 'a' been better fer yuh if yuh'd shot it out," sneered Blacksnake, "because Gentleman John will have somethin' in store fer yuh that yuh won't like. Wait till he sets eyes on yuh, Cotton-picker! Boilin' alive will seem like a picnic! I knew we'd get yuh sooner or later, if yuh kept stickin' yore nose in other folks' business."

"Blacksnake," said The Kid softly, "yo're a cheap, fo'-flushin' bully."

Blacksnake's evil eyes went hard. His face reddened with anger, then paled. He was trembling with fury and deadly hate. He turned to his men.

"Take the others up to the Yellow Houses and wait for me there," he rasped. "Pedro, my whip's on my pony;

bring it to me. I'm havin' this out with Cotton-picker, alone! When I'm through with him, I'll bring him on up. One of yuh ride up to the herd and tell Slim to let Gentleman John know we've got 'em. He'll finish with Cotton-picker when I'm done with him. Savvy?"

A blacksnake was brought to McCoy, and the others roughly surrounded Lefty and Red, herding them through the timber and out of sight.

"Take the skin off'n him, Black!" an outlaw yelled back.

The others laughed. And then Kid Wolf and his captor were left alone.

CHAPTER XIX

THE FANG OF THE WOLF

"Well, yuh'd better get ready to take yore medicine," sneered the outlaw, his voice shaking with rage. "I'm goin' to make yuh crawl on yore hands and knees, Cotton-picker!"

He holstered his gun, watching Kid Wolf cunningly, and drew back a little to give himself leeway with his whip. Then he began to roll up his sleeve.

"I'll make yuh beg, Cotton-picker," he taunted insultingly, as he bared his brawny right arm. "And if yuh run, I'll shoot—not to kill; that'd be too easy. I'll blow yore legs in two!"

Kid Wolf had been pulled from his horse by the

others, and the faithful snow-white animal had been taken along up the pass with the two prisoners. There seemed no way of escape. Blacksnake had him, and the gang leader grinned confidently.

"Yo're a bully, sah," drawled the Texan. It was as if he were deliberately trying to get his enemy aroused to white-hot fury.

The words seemed to have that effect. With a loud oath, Blacksnake cracked his whip like a pistol shot. The whip was as strong and tough as a bull whip, with a loaded stock and a long, braided lash, thick in the middle, like a snake. The outlaw had aimed for The Kid's thigh, and he was an expert with it. The lash landed with such cutting force that it cut through the Texan's clothing and tore into his flesh.

"Now take off yore shirt!" Blacksnake bellowed. "I'm goin' to flay yuh alive! Take it off!"

There was no sign of pain in Kid Wolf's face. He was still smiling agreeably. Blacksnake McCoy did not know what was coming. The Texan was not entirely disarmed. True, his Colts had been taken away, and he was apparently helpless. The Kid, however, had his hole card that was always in the deck. This was his keen bowie knife, which more than once had saved his life. Cleverly concealed in its sheath sewn down the back of his shirt collar, it had been overlooked in the outlaws' quick search. Pretending to remove his shirt, The Kid's right hand went to his throat and closed on the handle of the knife.

Blacksnake, showing his teeth in a laugh of hate,

stood a half dozen feet away from him, swinging his cruel whip slowly from side to side, waiting. He was holding the whipstock in his right hand, and that favored the Texan. For in order to draw the gun that swung at his hip, Blacksnake would first have to drop his implement of torture.

"Heah's wheah yo' get it!" snapped The Kid crisply.

Blacksnake's eyes bulged with sudden, startled terror, for he had a glimpse of the shining blade for one brief instant. His whip hand moved toward the butt of his gun. But he was too late. Kid Wolf could draw and throw his bowie as swiftly as he could pull his firearms. It flashed through the air—a streak of dazzling light! The fang of the wolf was striking!

Ping! The steel tore its way through the outlaw's right wrist. The Texan's throw had been as true as a rifle bead. Blacksnake yelled and tried to reach for his Colt with his left hand.

Then The Kid leaped in. Blacksnake was still squirming about and clawing for his .45 when the Texan's first blow landed. Blacksnake was burly, powerful. He weighed well over two hundred, and his shoulders were as broad as a gorilla's. But his bullet head went back with a jerk, as the Texan's hard fist thudded heavily on his cheek bone.

In the quick scuffle, the Big Colt slipped from Blacksnake's holster and fell to the ground. With all his fury now, the outlaw was lashing terrific, belting swings at Kid Wolf's head. The Texan dodged, elusive as a shadow. He leaped in, bored with his right and jolted

Blacksnake from top to toe with a smashing left. The big outlaw staggered, then jumped back and tried to scoop up his gun. His right hand was helpless, however, and his left clumsy. His fingers missed it, and The Kid hit him again, bringing Blacksnake to his knees, groggy-headed and bleary-eyed. His hand closed over the whip. The stock was heavily loaded with lead, and it was a terrible weapon when held reversed. One blow from it could crush a skull like an eggshell.

"I'm a-goin' to brain yuh, Cotton-picker!" Blacksnake grated furiously.

He reeled to his feet, shook his head to get his tangled hair out of his eyes and came in, whip swung back! Kid Wolf had no time to duck down for the gun. The heavy stock was humming through the air in a swish of death!

Smash! Blacksnake rocked on his feet. His teeth had come together with a click. He wabbled, swayed. His whip fell from his relaxed fingers. The Kid's footwork had been as swift and cunning as a mountain cat's! He had stepped aside, rocked his body in a pivot from the hips and landed a knockout punch full on the point of the big-chested outlaw's jaw! With a grunt, Blacksnake went down, first to his knees, and then face thudding the ground. He landed with such force that he plowed the sand with his nose like a rooting hog.

Taking a deep breath, Kid Wolf walked over and picked up Blacksnake's .45. Then he turned the outlaw face up, none too gently, by jerking his tangled hair. "All right. Snap out of it," he drawled.

Blacksnake was out for a full two minutes. Gradually

consciousness began to show on his ugly, bruised face. He stared at the Texan, blinking his eyes in bewilderment.

"Blast yuh!" he said thickly, when he could speak. "Guess yuh got me, Cotton-picker. I don't know yet how yuh done it."

He tried to seize the gun, but The Kid was too quick for him.

"None o' that," he drawled. "Get up! Yo're takin' me to the othahs. Move pronto to the Yellow Houses!"

A cunning look mingled with the hate in Blacksnake's swollen eyes.

"They'll kill yuh," he sneered. "Yuh ain't out o' this yet, blast yuh! My men will pull yuh to pieces."

"I'm thinkin' they won't." The Texan smiled. "If they do, it won't be very healthy fo' yo'. Now listen to what I say."

Half an hour later, Kid Wolf strolled up the hill to the Yellow Houses, arm in arm with his enemy—Blacksnake McCoy!

The outlaw was swearing under his breath. Kid Wolf was chuckling. For he had his hand under Blacksnake's vest, and that hand held a .45! In his left hand, the outlaw carried his whip. The other, wounded, was in his trousers pocket. The Texan had ordered him to keep it there, out of sight.

The two adobes, crumbling to ruins, dated from the Spaniards. For many years they had been used only as occasional stopping places for passing riders. It was here that Blacksnake had ordered Red Morton and Lefty Warren taken.

Kid Wolf was free now, and had he wished, he could have made his escape. That thought, however, did not enter the Texan's mind. He must rescue his friends if possible.

"Walk with me as if nothing had happened," he told Blacksnake softly. "If they suspect anything befo' I'm ready fo' 'em to know, you'll be sorry."

With the cold end of the six-gun pressing his ribs inside his shirt, the outlaw dared not disobey.

The sun had set, and twilight was deepening. The faint dust haze on the far horizon had disappeared. That meant that the stolen Diamond D herd had been driven on. Blacksnake had been staying some distance in the rear to keep off any possible pursuit. Kid Wolf had five other outlaws to contend with—no, four. For Blacksnake had sent one of them ahead with the herd.

Odds meant nothing, however, to the Texan. He knew that surprise and quick action always counted more than numbers. Everything now depended on boldness. As they neared the two adobes, he pretended to reel and stagger close against Blacksnake for support, as if he had been beaten until he could hardly stand. This, too, allowed him to keep the gun against the outlaw's side without arousing suspicion.

At the edge of the little cleared space surrounding the two adobes, one of the bandits was saddling a horse. The others seemed to be inside with the prisoners.

"Hello, Black!" the outlaw yelled. "Did yuh tear the

hide off'n him? From his looks, I reckon yuh did."

"Tell him to go inside," murmured Kid Wolf softly, "and be careful how yo' tell him."

Blacksnake opened his lips to shout a warning, but felt the touch of steel against his ribs and quickly changed his mind.

"Go into the 'dobe with the others," he commanded gruffly.

The walls of one of the mud huts had crumbled utterly. Only one of them was habitable, and it was to this one that the outlaw went, with Blacksnake and Kid Wolf following close behind. A yell greeted Blacksnake's arrival with his supposed prisoner.

"I thought yuh'd have to carry him back, Black, or drag him by the heels," one voice shouted. "Yuh must've got tired."

The time for action was at hand! The Kid and the outlaw stood framed for a brief second in the doorway. The Texan's eyes swept the room. The four outlaws were lazing comfortably about the ruined interior. Two were playing cards, and two were engaged in taking a drink from a whisky flask, one of these being the man Blacksnake had sent inside. The two prisoners—Lefty Warren and young Morton—were securely bound in lariat rope, sitting against one wall. The Kid saw their eyes light up as they recognized him. Evidently they had not expected to see him again alive. Kid Wolf jerked the revolver from Blacksnake's side, tripped him suddenly and sent him headlong into the room.

"Up with yo' hands!" the Texan sang out.

The outlaws were taken entirely by surprise. Only Blacksnake had known what was coming, and he was unarmed. Kid Wolf was no longer reeling and staggering. The desperadoes looked up to stare into the sinister muzzle of a .45!

"Shoot him to pieces!" Blacksnake yelled, picking himself up on all fours and whirling to make a jump for The Kid's ankles.

The Texan dodged to one side, his gun sweeping the room. A jet flame darted from the barrel, and there was a crash of broken glass. He had fired at the liquor flask that one of the outlaws still held at his lips.

"That's a remindah," he said crisply. "Put up yo' hands!"

Guns blazed suddenly. Two of the bandits had reached for their weapons at the same moment. The walls of the adobe shook under blended explosions, and powder smoke drifted down like a curtain, turning the figures of the men into drifting shadows.

The firing was soon over. The Kid's gun had roared a swift tattoo of hammering shots. Dust flew from the wall near his head, but he had spoiled the aim of both outlaws by fast, hair-trigger shooting. One sank against a broken-down bunk in one corner, reamed through the upper right arm and chest. The other fired again, but his gun hand was dangling, and he missed by a foot. Playing cards were scattered, as the other pair of bandits jumped up with their hands over their heads.

"We got enough!" they yelped. "Don't shoot!"

Kid Wolf lashed out at Blacksnake, who was rushing

him again. The short, powerful blow to the jaw sent the leader down for good. He rolled over, stunned.

"*Bueno.*" The Texan smiled. "Keep yo' hands right theah, please, caballeros."

Before the powder fumes had cleared away, he had liberated Lefty and Red with quick strokes of his bowie.

"I reckon we've got the uppah hand now, boys." He smiled. "Let's try and keep it. Take their guns, Red."

The two Diamond D men had been as surprised as the outlaws had been. They had watched the gun fight fearfully and hopefully, and it was an enthusiastic pair that shook off their severed bonds to clap The Kid across the back. There was no time for conversation now, however, and they busied themselves with disarming their five prisoners and binding them with rope.

"Gee, Kid!" Red whistled. "We thought we were done, and when yuh came in and made sparks fly—whew!"

"Theah'll be moah spahks fly, I'm afraid," the Texan drawled. "How'd yo' like to make some spahks fly yo'-selves?"

The others showed their eagerness. The fighting fever was in their veins, especially since the death of poor Mike Train. And now, with Blacksnake and half the outlaw gang captured, they felt that they had a good part of the battle won. Red tried to question Blacksnake about his brother's death, but the outlaw was stubborn and refused to talk. Had it not been for Kid Wolf, Red would have fallen on his enemy and beaten him with

196

his fists. And none of them could blame him.

It was nearly dark, and they made quick plans. The stolen herd was not far ahead, and with it were not more than seven of Gentleman John's riders.

"We'll take those cattle away from 'em," said Red fiercely, "and head the steers back to the Diamond D!"

It was decided that the prisoners could be left where they were for the time being, although Lefty Warren was for stringing them up there and then. Kid Wolf shook his head at this suggestion, however, and they armed themselves, "borrowing" the guns of the Black-snake gang. Then they mounted their horses and headed south through the deepening dusk.

CHAPTER XX

BATTLE ON THE MESA

"Oh, the cowboy sings so mournful on the Rio!
    To the dark night herd, so mournful and so
        sad,
And I'd like to be in the moonlight on the Rio,
    Wheah good men are good, and bad men are
        bad!"

K id Wolf sang the tune softly to the whispering wind, as the trio climbed under a New Mexican moon to the top of a vast mesa.

"Guess yuh'll find some plenty bad ones here in

Skull County, eh, Kid?" laughed Red grimly.

The Texan, brightly outlined on his beautiful horse in the moonlight, looked like a ghost on a moving white shadow.

"Bad men," mused Kid Wolf, "aren't so plentiful. Usually theah's some good in the blackest. The men we're goin' to fight tonight, fo' instance, are probably just driftahs who've drifted the wrong way. But Gentleman John—well, he's one of the few really bad men I've met. He's really the one we want."

The splendor of the night had a sobering effect on them. To be thinking of possible bloodshed in all that dream beauty seemed terrible. Yet it was necessary. It was a hard land. A man had to be his own law. And in Kid Wolf's case, he had to be the law for others, in a fight for the weak against the strong.

"Listen!" cried Lefty suddenly.

"And look!" whispered Red. "See those black dots against the sky over there? And there's a camp fire, too."

He was right. The glow of a fire reddened the horizon and the distant bawling of uneasy cattle could be heard on the night wind.

The rustlers had made a camp on the mesa until the dawn. The big herd was shifting, restless and milling.

"A gun fight will stampede that herd," observed Red.

"Then," said The Kid, "we'll be sure to stampede them in the right direction. Let's make a wide circle heah."

They rode to the west, so that they would not be outlined against the moon. A full, curving mile slipped under their horses' pounding hoofs before The Kid gave the signal for the turn. He had the outlaws spotted, every one, and all depended now on his generalship. He knew that the two riders on the far side of the night herd would be out of it—for the time, at least. When the herd started their mad stampede toward the Diamond D, they would have a high time just taking care of themselves. The others, five in number, would be dealt with first.

The trio slipped closer as silently as moving phantoms. The Kid saw three mounted men—two blocking their path, and the other on the far wing. Two other outlaws were at the fire. The Texan sniffed and smiled. They were making coffee.

"The two at the fiah make excellent tahgets," murmured Kid Wolf. "I'll leave them to yo', Red. Lefty, start now and ride toward the fah ridah. I'll try mah hand with these two. We'll count to fifty, Lefty; that'll give yo' time to get in range of yo' man. And then I'll give the coyote yell, and we'll start ouah little row. Don't kill unless necessary, but if they show fight, shoot fast."

Lefty grinned in the moonlight, roweled his horse lightly and drifted. Red and the Texan waited—ten seconds—twenty—thirty—forty—

"Yipee yip-yipee-ee!" The coyote cry rose, mournful and lonely.

Then came a terrific rattle of gunfire, with the dull drum of horses' hoofs as a bass accompaniment. Red spurred his horse toward the fire, shouting his battle cry and throwing down on the two startled men who leaped to their feet, reaching for their guns. Kid Wolf's great white charger burned the breeze at the two guards on the west wing.

"Throw up yo' hands!" The Kid invited.

But they didn't. Lead began to hum viciously. Bending low in their saddles, they drew and opened up a splattering fire. Their guns winked red flashes.

Lefty's man had shown fight, Lefty had bowled him over with a double trigger pull, and Lefty came racing back to help Red with the two rustlers at the camp fire.

There were fireworks, and plenty of them! The herd, mad with fear, started moving away—a frantic rush that became a wild stampede. Their plunging bodies milled about, and with uplifted tails and tossing horns, they were on the run northward toward the home range—the Diamond D!

Although it was a case of shoot or be killed now, The Kid was aiming to cripple. A leaden slug burned a flesh wound just below his left armpit, as he opened up on the two rustlers. His gun hammers stuttered down, throwing bullets on both sides of him, as he drove Blizzard between his two enemies at full tilt. One, raked with lead through both shoulders, thudded from his pony to the ground. The other leaned over his saddle and dropped his Colt. Two bullets, a few inches apart, had nipped his gun arm.

The two rustlers at the fire were giving trouble. They had dashed out of the dangerous firelight and had opened up on Lefty and Red. Kid Wolf's heart gave a little jump. Red was down! Lefty and one of the bandits were engaged in a hand-to-hand scuffle, for Warren's horse had been shot under him. The other outlaw had lifted his gun to finish Red, who was crawling along the ground. The range was a good fifty yards, but Kid Wolf fired three times. The rustler standing over Red dropped. Lefty broke away from his man, just as The Kid rode up with lariat swinging.

"Don't shoot!" the Texan sang out. "I've got him!"

The rope hummed through the air, spread out and tightened. The last of the outlaws went off his feet with a jerk.

"One of 'em's runnin' away!" yelled Lefty, pointing to the man Kid Wolf had shot through the arm. He was making a hot race in the direction of Skull.

"Let him go," said The Kid. "We don't want him. See how bad Red's hurt."

Outlined against the eastern sky were three riders now, far away and becoming rapidly smaller. The two north riders were making their getaway, also. The victory was complete.

To their relief, Lefty and The Kid found that Red had received only a flesh wound above the knee.

Kid Wolf tied the man he had caught with his lariat, then caught Red's horse and one of the loose outlaw ponies for Lefty.

"Now yo' ought to be able to ease those Diamond D cattle on home," he drawled. "I'll see how yo' are makin' it in the mo'ning."

"Why, where are yuh goin'?" Red asked in surprise.

"Goin' after Gentleman John." Kid Wolf smiled. "How far is it to his headquartahs at Agua Frio?"

"About nine miles straight west, over the mesa. But say, yuh'd better let one of us go with yuh."

The Texan shook his head. "I'm playin' a lone hand, Red. Yo' job is to line out yo' steers and get 'em back to the Diamond D feedin' grounds. Adios, amigos!"

And Kid Wolf, on his fleet white horse, swung off to the westward.

Gentleman John sat up suddenly in his bed and opened his eyes. The moon had gone down, and all was pitch dark. It was nearly morning.

He had heard something—for Gentleman John was a light sleeper. He listened intently, then sat on the edge of his bed to draw on his boots. The sound came again from the direction of the patio. Had his man, José, forgotten to lock the gate? Surely he had heard the chain rattling! Some horse, no doubt, or possibly a mule, had strayed into the little courtyard. Perhaps it was some of his men returning. And yet hardly that, for they would not dare disturb him at such an hour, but would go to their quarters behind the house until daybreak. Tiptoeing to the door, he put his ear to it. He heard faint noises, as if some one were moving about.

"José!" Gentleman John called angrily. "What are yuh fumblin' at in there? What's the matter? *Me oye usted?*"

There was no reply, and Gentleman John went to one corner of his room, scratched a sulphur match, and with

202

its sputtering flame he lighted a small lamp by his bedside. Then he slyly drew a derringer from under his pillow. Again he went to the door, putting his hand on the knob.

"José! Come here!" he cried, with an oath.

The door swung open, and the lamplight shone on a human face—a face that was not José's, but a stern white one with glinting blue eyes!

"José can't come," said a voice in a soft drawl. "He's tied up. But if I will do as well, I am at yo' service, sah!"

The color fled from Gentleman John's amazed face.

"Kid Wolf!" he almost screamed, and at the words he whirled up his black and ugly double-barreled pistol!

Span-ng-g-g-g! Br-r-rang! Both barrels of the derringer exploded in two quick roars. The leaden balls, however, went wild. A steel hand had closed lightning-swift on Gentleman John's right wrist.

"Be careful," the Texan mocked. "Yo' almost put out the lamp."

A terrific wrench made the bones pop in the cattle king's hand, and with a yell of pain he let go. Kid Wolf took the derringer, empty now, and tossed it contemptuously to one side.

"I'm ashamed of yo'," he drawled, with a slow smile. "Yo' ought to know bettah than to use a toy like that. Sit down on the bed, sah. I have a few things to say to yo'."

In his left hand The Kid held a big Colt .45. Gentleman John obeyed.

"My men will kill yuh fer this!" he raged.

"Yo' haven't any men, sah. They're done. And now yo' are done." Kid Wolf rolled a cigarette and lighted it over the lamp chimney. "Gentleman John," he drawled, "whoevah named yo' suah had a sense of humah. Yo' are a murderah, and a cowardly one, because yo' have othahs do yo' dirty work."

"Kill me and get it over!" jerked Gentleman John.

"Really, yo' shouldn't judge me by what yo' would do yo'self undah the circumstances," said The Kid mildly. "I'm not heah to kill yo'. I'm heah to take yo' back to Skull fo' trial and punishment."

"Fer trial!" repeated the cattle king. "Why, there ain't any law—"

"I hope yo' don't think," drawled the Texan, "that I wasted the time I spent in town. Theah's a new cattlemen's organization theah—and they've decided on drastic measures."

"Yuh can't prove a thing!" Gentleman John shot at him loudly.

The Kid raised his eyebrows.

"No?" he said softly. "Yo' men slipped up a little and left evidence when they murdahed Joe Morton. They left the bill o' sale he wouldn't sign! It'll go hahd with yo', but I'm givin' yo' one chance."

Kid Wolf glanced around the room, and his eyes fell on paper and pen near the lamp. Placing his gun at his elbow, within easy reach, the Texan wrote steadily for a full minute. Then he turned and handed the cattle king the slip of paper.

"Yo' through in Nueva Mex, Gentleman John," The

Kid drawled. "It's just a question of who falls heir to yo' holdin's. Read that ovah."

The cattle king read it. It was brief, but to the point:

I, Gentleman John, do hereby give and hand over all my estates, land, holdings, and live stock to Red Morton, of Skull County, New Mexico, for consideration received.

"Theah's a bill o' sale fo' yo' to sign." The Texan smiled grimly.

"If I sign under pressure, it won't hold good," blustered Gentleman John.

"Yo' won't be in this country to contest it," Kid Wolf drawled. "This won't in any way repay Red fo' the loss of his brothah, but it's something. Yo' can do as yo' like about signin' it."

"Then of course I won't sign!" snarled the other.

"The honest cattlemen at Skull will probably hang yo'," reminded The Kid softly.

Beads of sweat suddenly stood out on Gentleman John's forehead. His own guilty conscience told him that what The Kid said was true. His gimlet eyes grew big with fear. There was a long silence.

"If—if I sign, yo'll let me go?" he quavered.

The Texan's face grew hard and stern.

"No," he said. "I haven't any right to do that. Justice demands that yo' face the ones yo' have wronged. And justice has always been my guidin' stah. I'm a soldier of misfohtune, fightin' fo' the undah dawg.

I'm takin' yo' to Skull, sah."

Gentleman John groaned in terror. All the blustering bravado had gone out of him.

"I can't promise yo' yo' life," Kid Wolf went on. "I can, howevah, recommend banishment instead of death, and mah word carries some weight in Skull, undah the new ordah of things. If yo' sign—thus doin' right by Red Morton, whom yo' wronged—I'll do what I can to save yo' from the rope, but I can't promise that yo'll escape it. Are yo' signin'?"

Gentleman John moistened his lips feverishly, and his hand trembled as he reached for the pen.

"I'll sign," he groaned.

When he had scratched his signature, Kid Wolf took the paper, folded it carefully and put it in his pocket.

"Bueno," he said softly. "Now get yo' hat and coat. I hate to rob yo' of yo' sleep, but I have some othah pris-onahs to round up tonight."

And while binding Gentleman John's wrists, Kid Wolf hummed a new verse to his favorite tune, "On the Rio."

CHAPTER XXI

APACHES

In the half light of the early morning, a stagecoach was rattling down a steep hill near the New Mexico-Arizona boundary line. The team of six bronchos fought against the weight of the lumbering vehicle behind, with stiff front legs threw themselves back against their harness. The driver, high on his box, sawed at the lines with his foot heavy on the creaking brake.

"Whoa!" he roared. "Easy, yuh cow-faced loco-eyed broncs! Steady now, or I'll beat the livin' tar outn yuh!"

The ponies seemed to disregard his bellowing abuse. They had heard it before, and knew that he didn't mean a word he said. They were almost at the foot of the hill now, and the thick white dust, kicked up in choking spurts by the rumbling wheels, sifted down on the leathery mesquite and dagger plants below.

"I don't like the looks o' that brush down there," said the other man on the box. He was an express guard, and across his knees was a sawed-off shotgun loaded with buckshot.

"Perfect place fer an ambush, ain't it?" admitted the driver. "Well, if the Apaches do git us, I will say they'll make a nice haul."

It was a dangerous time on the great Southwest frontier. Law had not yet come to that savage country of flaming desert and baking mountain. Even a worse peril than the operations of the renegades and bad men of the border was the threat of the Apaches. Behind any clump of mesquites a body of these grim and terrible fighters of the arid lands might lurk, eager for murder and robbery. And it was rumored that a chief even more cruel than Geronimo, Cochise, or Mangus Colorado was at their head.

The men who operated the stage line knew the risk

they were taking in that unbroken country, but they were of the type that could look danger in the face and laugh. The two steely-eyed men on the coach box, this gray morning, were samples of the breed.

Inside the vehicle were four passengers. Three of them were men past middle life—miners and cattlemen. The third was a youth who addressed one of the older men as "father." All were armed with six-guns, and all were bound for the valley of San Simon.

The stage had reached the bottom of the hill now, and as the team reached the level ground, the driver lined them out and settled back in his seat with a satisfied grunt. About both sides of the trail at this point grew great thickets of brush—paloverde, the darker mesquites, and grotesque bunches of prickly pear. One of the bronchos suddenly reared backward.

"Steady, yuh ornery—" the driver began.

He did not finish. There was a sharp *twang!* An arrow whistled out of the mesquites and buried itself in the side of the coach nearly to the feather! As if this were a signal, a dozen rifles cracked out from the brush. Bowstrings snapped, and a shower of arrows and lead hummed around the heads of the frightened ponies. The driver cried out in pain as a bullet hit his leg.

"Apaches!" the express guard yelled, throwing up his sawed-off shotgun.

Two streaks of red fire darted through the haze of black powder smoke as he fired both barrels into the brush. The driver recovered himself, seized the reins and began to "pour leather" onto his fear-crazed team.

With drawn guns, the four passengers in the coach waited for something to shoot at. They were soon to see plenty.

The mesquites suddenly became alive with brown-skinned warriors, hideous with paint and screaming their hoarse death cry. Some were mounted, and others were on foot. All charged the coach.

There must have been fifty in the swarm, and still they came! Those that were armed with rifles fired madly into the coach and at the team. Others rushed up and tried to seize the bridles.

"It's all up with us!" the guard cried, drawing his big .45 Colt.

"But we ain't—goin' to sell out—cheap!" the driver panted.

Escape was impossible now, for two of the horses went down, plunging and kicking at the harness in their death agony. The other animals—some wounded, and all of them mad with fright—overturned the old stage-coach. With a loud crash, the vehicle went over on its side! The driver and guard, teeth bared in grins of fury, raised their six-guns and prepared to sell their lives as dearly as possible. The passengers inside began firing desperately.

The renegade Indians rushed. They nearly gained the wrecked stage, but not quite. Before the straight shooting of the trapped whites, they fell back to cover again. They did not believe in taking unnecessary chances. They had their victims where they wanted them, and it would be only a question of time before they would be slaughtered. The fight became a siege.

It was sixty against six—or, rather, it was sixty to five. For the redskins had increased the odds by shooting down the driver. The second bullet he received drilled him through the heart. The guard, scrambling for shelter, joined the four men in the overturned coach.

The Apaches, back in their refuge among the brush, began playing a waiting game. The fire, for a moment, ceased.

"They'll rush again in a minute," muttered the guard. "We'll do well to stop 'em. Anyways, we won't hold out long. Just a question o' time."

"Is there any chance o' help?" asked one of the men, while loading his revolver.

He was a broad-shouldered, big-chested man of fifty—the father of the youth who was now fighting beside him.

The guard shook his head. "Afraid not. Unless one of us could get through to Lost Springs, six miles from here. Even if we could, I don't think we'd get any help. There's not many livin' there, and they're all scared of Apaches. Can't say I blame 'em."

Bullets began to buzz again. The Indians were making another charge. A dense cloud of smoke hung over the ambushed coach. White powder spurts blossomed out from the brush, and the war cry came shrilly. The rush brought a line of half-naked warriors to within a few yards of the coach. Then they fell back again, leaving four of their number dead or wounded on the sand.

"So far, so good," panted the guard. "But we can't do that forever!"

The youngest of the party, pale of face but determined, spoke up quickly:

"I'm willin' to take the chance o' gettin' to Lost Springs," he said.

"Yuh can't make it alive through that bunch o' devils," the guard told him.

"It's our only chance," the other returned. "I'm goin' to try. Good-by, dad!"

It was a sad, heart-wrenching moment. There was small chance that the two would ever see each other alive again. But father and son shook hands and passed it over with a smile.

"Good luck, son!"

And then the younger one slipped out of the coach and was gone.

The others watched breathlessly. This movement had taken the savages by surprise. The lad darted into the mesquites, running with head low. Bullets buzzed about him, kicking up clouds of dust at his feet. Arrows whistled after him. A yell went up from the Apaches.

"Will he make it?" groaned the father, in an agonized voice.

"Doubt it," said the guard.

The messenger sprinted at top speed through the brush, then dived down into an arroyo. A score of warriors swarmed after him, firing shot after shot from their rifles. Already the youth was out of arrow range.

The guard shaded his eyes with his hand. "He's got a

211

chance, anyways," he decided.

The town of Lost Springs—if such a tiny settlement could have been called a town—sprawled in a valley of cottonwoods, a scattering of low-roofed adobes. To find such an oasis, after traveling the heat-tortured wilderness to the east or the west, was such relief to the wayfarer that few missed stopping.

There was but one public building in the place—a large building of plastered earth which was at the same time a saloon, a store, a gambling hall, and a meeting place for those who cared to partake of its hospitality.

The crude sign over the narrow door read: "Garvey's Place." It was enough. Garvey was the storekeeper, the master of the gamblers, and the saloon owner. Lost Springs was a one-man town, and that man was Gil Garvey. His reputation was not of the best. Dark marks had been chalked up against his record, and his past was shady, too. There were whispers, too, of even worse things. It was, however, a land where nobody asked questions. It was too dangerous. Garvey was accepted in Lost Springs because he had power.

It was a hot morning. The thermometer outside Garvey's door already registered one hundred and five. Heat devils chased one another across the valley. But inside the building it was comparatively cool. Glasses tinkled on the long, smooth bar. The roulette wheel whirred, and even at that early hour, cards were being slapped down, faces up, at the stud-poker table. Including the customers at the bar, there were perhaps a dozen men in the house besides Garvey himself.

Garvey was tending bar, which was his habit until noon, when his bartender relieved him.

Gil Garvey was a menacing figure of a man, massive of build and sinister of face. His jet-black eyebrows met in the center of his scowling forehead, and under them gleamed eyes cold and dangerous. A thin wisp of a dark mustache contrasted with the quick gleam of his strong, white teeth. On the rare occasions when he laughed, his mirth was like the hungry snarl of a wolf.

The sprinkling of drinkers at the bar strolled over to watch the faro game, and Garvey, taking off his soiled apron, joined them, lighting a black cigar. The ruler of Lost Springs moved lightly on his feet for so heavy a man. Around his waist was a gun belt from which swung a silver-mounted .44 revolver in a beaded holster.

Suddenly a slim figure reeled through the open door, and with groping, outstretched arms, staggered forward.

"Apaches!" he choked.

Nearly every one leaped to his feet, hand on gun. Some rushed to the door for a look outside. A score of questions were fired at the newcomer.

"They're attackin' the stage at the foot of the pass!" explained the messenger.

There were sighs of relief at this bit of news, for at first they had thought that the red warriors were about to enter the town. But six miles away! That was a different matter.

"I'm Dave Robbins," the youth went on desperately.

"I've got to go back there with help. When I left, they were holdin' 'em off. Fifty or sixty Indians!"

Some of the saloon customers began to murmur their sympathy. But it was evident that they were none too eager to go to the aid of the ambushed stagecoach.

Young Robbins—covered with dust, his face scratched by cactus thorns, and with an arrow still hanging from his clothing—saw the indifference in their eyes.

"Surely yuh'll go!" he pleaded. "Yuh—yuh've got to! My father's in the coach!"

Garvey spoke up, smiling behind his mustache.

"What could we do against sixty Apaches?" he demanded. "Besides, the men in the stage are dead ones by this time. We couldn't do any good."

Robbins' face went white. With clenched fists, he advanced toward Garvey.

"Yo're cowards, that's all!" he cried. "Cowards! And yo're the biggest one of 'em all!"

Garvey drew back his huge arm and sent his fist crashing into the youth's face. Robbins, weak and exhausted as he was, went sprawling to the floor.

And at that moment the swinging doors of the saloon opened wide. The man who stood framed there, sweeping the room with cool, calm eyes, was scarcely older than the youth who had been slugged down. His rather long, fair hair was in contrast with the golden tan of his face. He wore a shirt of fringed buckskin, open at the neck. His trousers were tucked into silver-studded riding boots, weighted with spurs that jingled in tune to his swinging stride. At each trim hip was the butt of a .45 revolver.

The newcomer's eyes held the attention of the men in Garvey's Place. They were blue and mild, but little glinting lights seemed to sparkle behind them. He was silent for a long moment, and when he finally spoke, it was in a soft, deliberate Southern drawl:

"Isn't it rathah wahm foh such violent exercise, gentlemen?"

Robbins, crimsoned at the mouth, raised on one elbow to look at the stranger. Garvey's lips curled in a sneer.

"Are yuh tryin' to mind my business?" he leered.

"When I mind somebody else's business," said the young stranger softly, "that somebody else isn't usually in business any moah."

Garvey caught the other's gaze and seemed to find something dangerous there, for he drew back a step, content with muttering oaths under his breath.

"What's the trouble?" the stranger asked Robbins quietly.

The youth seemed to know that he had found a friend, for he at once told the story of the ambushed stage.

"I came here for help," he concluded, "and was turned down. These men are afraid to go. My—my father's on that stage. Won't you help me?"

The stranger seemed to consider.

"Sho'," he drawled at length, "I'll throw in with you." He paused to face the gathered company. "And these othah men are goin' to throw in with yo', too!"

The men in the saloon stood aghast, open-mouthed. But they didn't hesitate long. When the stranger spoke again, his words came like the crack of a whip:

"Get yo' hosses!"

Garvey's heavy-jawed face went purple with fury. That this young unknown dared to try such high-handed methods so boldly in Lost Springs—which he ruled—maddened him! His big hand slid down toward his hip with the rapidity of a lightning bolt.

There was a resounding crash—a burst of red flame. Garvey's hand never closed over his gun butt. The stranger had drawn and fired so quickly that nobody saw his arm move. And the reason that the amazed Garvey did not touch the handle of his .44 was because there was no handle there! The young newcomer's bullet had struck the butt of the holstered gun and smashed it to bits.

Garvey stared at the handleless gun as if stupefied. Then his amazed glance fell upon the stranger, who was smiling easily through the flickering powder fumes.

"Who—who are yuh?" he stammered.

The stranger smiled. "Kid Wolf," he drawled, "from Texas, sah. My friends simply say 'Kid,' but to my enemies I'm 'The Wolf'!"

CHAPTER XXII

THE RESCUE

The stranger's crisp words had their effect, since "Kid Wolf" was a name well known west of the Chisholm Trail. His reputation had been passed by word of mouth along the border until there were few who had not heard of his deeds. His very name seemed to fill the riffraff of the barroom with courage. Some of them cheered, and all prepared to obey the young Texan's orders. Every one was soon busy loading and examining six-guns.

Garvey was the one exception. He was infuriated, and his malignant eyes gleamed with hate. Kid Wolf had made an enemy. He was, however, accustomed to that. Smiling ironically, he faced Garvey, who was quivering all over with helpless rage.

"Yo' won't need to come along," he drawled. "I'd rathah have Apaches in front of me than yo' behind me."

Kid Wolf lost no time in rounding up his hastily drafted posse. A horse was procured for Robbins and The Kid prepared to ride by his side. Kid Wolf's horse was "tied to the ground" outside, and a shout of genuine admiration went up as the men caught sight of the magnificent creature, beautiful with muscular grace. Swinging into his California saddle, the Texan, with Robbins at his side and the posse, numbering eleven

217

men, swept down toward the mountain pass.

Some of the men carried Winchesters, but for the most part they were armed with six-guns. Now that they were actually on the way, the men seemed eager for the battle. Perhaps Kid Wolf's cool and determined leadership had something to do with it.

Young Robbins reached over and clasped the Texan's hand.

"I'll never forget this, Mr. Kid Wolf," he said, tears in his eyes. "If it wasn't for you—"

"Call me 'Kid,'" said the Texan, flashing him a smile. "We'll save yo' fathah and the men in the stage if we can. Anyway, we'll make it hot fo' those Apaches."

After a few minutes of fast going, they could hear the faint crackling of gunfire ahead of them, carried on the torrid wind. Robbins brightened, for this meant that some survivors still remained on their feet. Kid Wolf, experienced in Indian warfare, understood the situation at once, and ordered his men to scatter and come in on the Indians from all sides.

"Robbins," he said, "I want yo' with me. Yo' two," he went on, singling out a couple of the posse, "ride in from the east. The rest of yo' come in from the west and south. Make every shot count, fo' if we don't scattah the Apaches at the first chahge, we will be at a big disadvantage!"

It was a desperate situation, with the odds nearly five to one against them. Reaching the pass, they could look down on the battle from the cover of the mesquites.

From the overturned stage, thin jets of fire streaked steadily, and a pall of white smoke hung over it like a cloud. From the brush, other gun flashes answered the fire. Occasionally a writhing brown body could be seen, crawling from point to point. The thicket seemed to be alive with them.

Kid Wolf listened for a moment to the faint popping of the guns. Then he raised his hand in a signal.

"Let's go!" he sang out.

A second later, Blizzard was pounding down the pass like a snowstorm before the wind.

The leader of this band of murderous Apaches was a youthful warrior named Bear Claw, the son of the tribal chief. Peering at the coach from his post behind a clump of paloverde, his cruel face was lighted by a grin of satisfaction. From time to time he gave a hoarse order, and at his bidding, his braves would creep up or fall back as the occasion demanded.

Bear Claw was in high good humor, for he saw that the ambushed victims in the stage could not hope to hold out much longer. Only three remained alive in the coach, and some of these were wounded. The white men's fire was becoming less accurate.

The young leader of the Apaches was horrible to look at. He was naked save for a breechcloth and boot moccasins and his face was daubed with ocher and vermilion. Across his lean chest, too, was a smear of paint just under the necklace of bear claws that gave him his name. He was armed with a .50-caliber Sharps single-shot rifle and with the only revolver in the tribe—an old-fashioned cap-and-ball six-shooter, taken from some murdered prospector.

Bear Claw was about to raise his left hand—a signal for the final rush that would wipe out the white men in the overturned coach—when a terrific volley burst out like rattling thunder from all sides. Bullets raked the brush in a deadly hail. An Indian a few paces from Bear Claw jumped up with a weird yell and fell back again, pierced through the body.

The young chief saw whirlwinds of dust swooping down on the scene from every direction. In those whirlwinds, he knew, were horses. Bear Claw had courage only when the odds were with him. How many men were in the attacking force, he did not know. But there were too many to suit him, and he took no chances. He gave the order for retreat, and the startled Apaches made a rush for their ponies, hidden in an arroyo. Bear Claw scrambled after them, with lead kicking up dust all about him.

But it did not take Bear Claw long to see that his band outnumbered the white posse, more than four to one. Throwing himself on his horse, he decided to set his renegade warriors an example. Giving the Apache war whoop, he kicked his heels in his pony's flanks and led the charge. Picking out the foremost of the posse—a bronzed rider on a snow-white horse—he went at him with leveled revolver.

What happened then unnerved the Apaches at Bear Claw's back. The man Bear Claw had charged was Kid Wolf! The Texan did not return the Indian's blaze of revolver fire. He merely ducked low in his saddle and swung his big white horse into Bear Claw's pony! At the same time, he swung out his left hand sharply. It caught Bear Claw's jaw with a terrific jolt. The weight of both speeding horses was behind the impact. Something snapped. Bear Claw went off his pony's back like a bag of meal and landed on the sand, his head at a queer angle. His neck was broken!

Then Kid Wolf's guns began to talk. Fire burst from the level of both his hips as he put spurs to Blizzard and charged with head low directly into the amazed Apaches. The others, too, followed the Texan's example, but it was Kid Wolf who turned the trick. It was the deciding card, and without their chief, the redskins were panic-stricken. The only thing they thought of now was escape. The little hoofs of their ponies began to drum madly. But instead of rushing in the direction of the whites, they drummed away from them. Kid Wolf ordered his men not to follow. Nor would he allow any more firing.

"No slaughter, men," he said. "Save yo' bullets till yo' need them. Let's take a look at the stage."

Wheeling their mounts, the posse, who had lost not a man in the encounter, raced back to the overturned coach. The vehicle, riddled with bullets and arrows, resembled a butcher's shop. On the ground near it was the body of the driver, while the guard, hit in a dozen places, lay half in and half out of the coach, dead.

Young Robbins had left four men alive when he made his escape toward Lost Springs. There now remained only two. And one of these, it could be seen, was dying.

"Dad!" Robbins cried. "Are yuh hurt?"

"Got a bullet in the shoulder and one in the knee," replied his father, crawling out with difficulty. "Good thing yuh got here when yuh did! See to Claymore. He's hit bad. I'm all right."

Kid Wolf drew out the still breathing form of the other survivor. He was quick to note that the man was beyond any human aid. The frontiersman, his six-gun still emitting a curl of blue smoke, was placed in the shade of the coach, and water was given to him.

"I'm all shot to pieces, boys," he gasped. "I'm goin' fast—but I'm glad the Apaches won't have me to—chop up afterward. Take my word for it—there's some white man—behind this. There's twenty thousand dollars in the express box—"

His words trailed off, and with a moan, he breathed his last. Kid Wolf gently drew a blanket over his face and then turned to the others.

"I think he's right," he mused, as he took off his wide-brimmed hat. "When Indians murdah, theah's usually a white man's brains behind them."

Garvey, when Kid Wolf had left with his quickly gathered posse, went to the bar and took several drinks of his own liquor. It was a fiery red whisky distilled from wheat, and of the type known to the Indians as "fire water." It did not put Garvey in any better humor. Wiping his lips, he left his saloon and crossed the road to a tiny one-room adobe.

A young Indian was sleeping in the shade, and Garvey awakened him with a few well-directed kicks. The Indian's eyes widened with fear at the sight of the white man's rage-distorted face, and when he had heard his orders, delivered in the hoarse Apache tongue, he raced for his pony, tethered in the bushes near him, and drummed away.

"Tell 'em to meet me in the saloon pronto!" Garvey shouted after him.

The saloon keeper passed an impatient half hour. A quartet of Mexicans entered his place demanding liquor, but Garvey waved them away. Something important was evidently on foot.

Soon the dull *clip-clop* of horses' hoofs was heard, and he went to the door to see five riders approaching Lost Springs from the north. He waved his hand to them before they had left the cover of the cotton-woods.

The group of sunburned, booted men who hastily entered Garvey's Place were individuals of the Lost Springs ruler's own stamp. All were gunmen, and some wore two revolvers. Most of them were wanted by the law for dark deeds done elsewhere. Sheriffs from the Texas Panhandle would have recognized two of them as Al and Andy Arnold—brother murderers. Another was a killer chased out of Dodge City, Kansas—a slender, quick-fingered youth known as "Pick" Stephenson. Henry Shank—a gunman from Lincoln, New Mexico—strode in their lead.

The fifth member of the quintet was the most terrible of them all. He was a half-breed Apache, dressed partly in the Indian way and partly like a white. He wore a battered felt hat with a feather in the crown. He wore no shirt, but over his naked chest was buttoned a dirty vest, around which two cap-and-ball Colt revolvers swung.

His stride, muffled by his beaded moccasins, was as noiseless as a cat's. This man—Garvey's go-between— was Charley Hood. He grinned continually, but his smile was like the snarl of a snapping dog.

"What's up, Garvey?" Shank demanded. "We was just ready to start out fer a cattle clean-up."

"Plenty's up," snarled Garvey. "Help yoreselves to liquor while I tell yuh. First o' all, do any of yuh know Kid Wolf?"

It was evident that most of them had heard of him. None had seen him, however, and Garvey went on to tell what had happened.

"How many men did he take with him?" Stephenson wanted to know.

"About a dozen."

"Bear Claw will wipe him out, then," grinned Al Arnold.

"Somehow I don't think so," said Garvey. "And if that stage deal fails us—"

"A twenty-thousand-dollar job!" Shank barked angrily. "And we get half!"

"We get all," chuckled Garvey. "The Apaches will give their share to me for fire water. That's why this must go through. If Bear Claw and his braves slip up, we'll have to finish it. As for Kid Wolf—"

Garvey's expression changed to one of malignant fury, and he made the significant gesture of cutting a throat.

"I hear that this Kid Wolf makes it his business to right wrongs," Shank sneered. "Thinks he's a law of himself. Justice, he calls it."

"Well, one thing!" roared Garvey, thumping the bar. "There ain't no law west o' the Pecos! And he's west o' the Pecos now! The only law here is this kind," and he tapped his .44.

"What's happened to yore gun?" one of them asked.

Garvey's face suddenly went dark red.

"I dropped it this mornin' and busted the handle," he lied. "If it had been in workin' order, I'd have got this Kid Wolf the minute he opened his mouth."

"Well, if the Apaches don't get him, we will," Stephenson declared. "By the way, Garvey, there's another deal on foot. What do yuh think o' this?" And he laid a chunk of ore on the bar under the saloon keeper's nose.

"Solid silver!" Garvey gasped. "Where's it from?"

"From the valley of the San Simon. It's from land owned—owned, mind yuh—by an hombre named Robbins. Gov'ment grant."

"We'll figger a way to get it," returned Garvey, then his eyes narrowed. "What name did yuh say?"

"Robbins. Bill Robbins."

Garvey grinned. "Why, he was on the stage! It was his kid that came here and made his play fer help.

Looks like things is comin' our way, after all."

The conference was interrupted by the sound of galloping hoofs. An Indian pounded up in front of the saloon in a cloud of yellow dust. The pony was lathered and breathing hard.

"It's a scout!" Garvey cried. "Let him in, and we'll see what he has to say."

The Indian runner's words, gasped in halting, broken English, brought consternation to Garvey and his treacherous gunmen:

"No get money box. Have keel two-three, maybe more, of white men in stage wagon. Then riders come. White chief on white devil horse, he break Bear Claw's neck. Bear Claw die. We ride away as fast as could do. White men fix stage wagon. Hunt for horse to drive it to Lost Springs."

Garvey clenched his huge fists.

"Get me another gun!" he rasped. "We'll have this out with Kid Wolf right now!"

Charley Hood spoke for the first time, and his bestial face with distorted with rage.

"Bear Claw son of Great Chief Yellow Skull! Yellow Skull get Keed Wolf if he have to follow him across world! And when he get him—"

Charley Hood, the half-breed, laughed insanely.

"I never thought of that," said Garvey. "Maybe we'd be doin' Mr. Wolf from Texas a favor by puttin' lead through him. Bear Claw was Yellow Skull's favorite. The old chief is an expert at torture. I'd like to be on hand to see it. But I've got an idea. Shank, have José dig a grave on Boot Hill—make it two of 'em. We've got to get that express money."

"And the silver," chuckled the desperado, as he took a farewell drink at the bar.

CHAPTER XXIII

TWO OPEN GRAVES

I t was some time before the overturned stagecoach could be righted. It took longer to provide a team for it. When the bodies of the unfortunate white men had been loaded into the vehicle and the ponies lined out it was late in the afternoon.

Kid Wolf had examined the contents of the express box and found that it contained a small fortune in money. He decided to take charge of it and see that it reached proper hands. Twenty miles west of Lost Springs, he learned, were an express-company station and agent. The Texan planned to guard the money at Lost Springs overnight and then take it on to the express post, located at Mexican Tanks.

The two Robbinses, both father and son, were overcome with gratitude toward the man who had saved them. They at once agreed to stay with Kid Wolf.

The posse members that the Texan had drafted at revolver point were not so willing. Although most of them were honest men, they feared Garvey's gang and the consequences of their act. All of them suspected

227

that Garvey had a hand in the plot to rob the stage-coach. Most of them made excuses and rode away in different directions.

"We beat the Apaches," explained one, "so I reckon I'll go back to the ranch. Adios, and good luck!"

Kid Wolf smiled. He knew that the men were leaving him for other reasons. Perhaps a man with less courage would have avoided Lost Springs, or even abandoned the money. The young Texan, however, was not to be swerved from what he believed to be the right.

"Look out for Garvey, Kid," begged Dave Robbins. "He hates yuh for what yuh done."

"I've heard of him," the elder Robbins added. "If helpin' us has got you into trouble, I'm sorry. He's a man without a heart."

"Then some day," Kid Wolf said softly, "he's liable to find a bullet in the spot wheah his heart ought to be. I don't regret comin' to yo' aid, not fo' a minute. And I guess Blizzahd and I are ready to see this thing through to the end."

Kid Wolf was riding on his white horse alongside the rumbling stage. The only member of the drafted posse who had stayed was driving the vehicle, and beside him on the box rode the two Robbinses, father and son.

The road to Lost Springs was not the direct route the Indian messenger had taken. It led around steep side hills and high-banked washes in which nothing grew but tough, stunted clumps of thirsty paloverde. Near the tiny settlement, the trail climbed a long slope to swing around a cactus-cluttered mound which served as Lost

Springs' Boot Hill. The stage trail cut the barren little graveyard in two, and on both sides of it were head-boards, some rotting with age, and others quite new, marking the last resting places of men who had died with smoke in their eyes.

It was nearly sundown when Kid Wolf and the party with the bullet-riddled coach reached this point. They found a group of hard-eyed men waiting for them. With Garvey were his five gunmen, mounted, armed to the teeth, and blocking the road! Kid Wolf caught the driver's eyes and nodded for him to go on. The stage rumbled up to the spot where Garvey waited.

"Stop!" the Lost Springs ruler snarled. "I reckon we want some words with yuh!"

"Is it words yo' want," drawled the Texan, drawing up his snowy mount, "or bullets?"

"That depends on you!" Garvey snapped. "We mean business. Hand over that express money."

"And the next thing?" the Texan asked softly.

"Next thing, we got business with that man!" Garvey pointed to Dave Robbins' father.

"With me?" Robbins demanded in astonishment.

"The same. We want yuh to sign this paper, turnin' over yore claim in the San Simon to me. Now both of yuh have heard!"

"But why should yuh want my claim in San Simon?"

"Yuh might as well know," Garvey sneered in reply, "there's silver on it. And I want it. Hand over that express box now and sign the paper. If yuh don't—"

"And if we don't?" Kid Wolf asked mildly. His eyebrows had risen the merest trifle.

"Here's the answer!" Garvey rasped. He pointed at two mounds of freshly disturbed earth a few feet from the road. "Read what's written over 'em, and take yore choice."

Kid Wolf saw that two headboards had been erected near the shallow graves. One of them had the following significant epitaph written on it in neatly printed Spanish:

Aqui llacen restos de Kid Wolf.

This in English was translated: "Here lies in the grave, at rest, Kid Wolf."

The other headboard was the same, except that the name "Bill Robbins" had been inserted.

"Those graves will be filled," sneered Garvey, "unless yuh both come through. Now what's yore answer?"

"Garvey," spoke up Kid Wolf, "I've known of othah white men who hired the Apaches to do their dirty work. They all came to a bad end. And so, if yo' want my answah—take it!"

Garvey's gang found themselves staring into the muzzles of two .45s!

The draw had been magical, so swiftly had the Texan's hands snapped down at his hips. Al Arnold, alone of the six riders, saw the movement in time even to think about drawing his own weapon. And perhaps it would have been better if he had not seen, for his own gun pull was slow and clumsy in comparison with Kid Wolf's. His right hand had moved but a few inches when the Texan's left-hand Colt spat a wicked tongue of flame.

Before the thunder of the explosion could be heard, the leaden slug tore its way through Arnold's wrist. Before the puff of black powder smoke had drifted away, Arnold's gun was thudding to the ground. The others dared not draw, as Kid Wolf's other six-gun still swept them. They knew that the Texan could not fail to get one or more of them, and they hesitated. Garvey himself remained motionless, frozen in the saddle. His lips trembled with rage.

"I'm not a killah," Kid Wolf drawled. "I nevah take life unless it's forced on me. If I did, I'd soon make Lost Springs a bettah place to live in. Now turn yo' backs with yo' hands in the air—and ride! The next time I shoot, it's goin' to be on sight! Vamose! Pronto!"

Muttering angrily under their breath, Garvey and his gunmen obeyed the order. Yet Kid Wolf knew that the trouble had not been averted, but merely postponed. He was not through with the Lost Springs bandit gang.

The driver of the coach—the only member of the posse who had remained loyal in the face of peril—was a man of courage. Johnson was his name, and he offered his adobe house as a place of refuge for the night.

"I'm thinkin' yuh'll be needin' it," he told the Texan. "We can stand 'em off there, for a while, anyway.

Garvey will have a hundred Mexes and Injuns with him before mornin'."

Kid Wolf accepted, and the coach was deserted. They buried the bodies of the men they had brought in the stage, not in the Lost Springs graveyard, but in an arroyo near it. Then they removed the valuable express box and took it with them to the Johnson adobe.

The house was a two-room affair, not more than a quarter of a mile from the Springs, and still closer to Boot Hill. On the side next to the water hole, the grass and tulles grew nearly waist-high. On the other three sides, barren ground swept out as far as eye could reach.

Kid Wolf placed the express box in the one living room of the hut. As a great deal might depend upon having horses ready, Blizzard, along with two pinto ponies, was quartered in the other apartment. This done, and with one of the four men standing watch at all times, they prepared a hasty meal.

"One thing we lack that we got to have," stated Johnson. "It's water. I'll take a bucket and go to the spring. I know the path through the tulles."

They watched him proceed warily toward the water hole. The landscape was peaceful. Not a moving thing could be seen. In a few moments, Johnson was swallowed up in the high grass. He reappeared again, carrying a brimming bucket. They could see the setting sun sparkling on the water as he swung along. Then suddenly a shot rang out sharply—the unmistakable crack of a Sharps .50-caliber rifle! Without a cry,

Johnson sank into the tulles, the bucket clattering beside him. He had been shot in the back!

A cry of horror burst from the lips of the watchers in the adobe. It was all that Kid Wolf could do to hold back the excitable younger Robbins, who wanted to avenge their friend's death immediately.

"No use fo' us to show ouahselves until we know how the cahds are stacked," the Texan said grimly. "Nevah mind, Dave. They'll pay fo' it!"

It was hard to tell just how many of their enemies might be lurking in the tulles or beyond them. They were soon to find that there were far too many. Gunfire began to blaze out in sharp, reëchoing volleys. Bullets clipped the adobe shack, sending up spurts of gray dust.

"Don't show yo'selves," Kid Wolf warned.

His keen eyes lined out the sights of his own twin Colts, and he fired twice, and then twice again. As far as the others could see, there was nothing in view to shoot at; but agitated threshings about in the tulles showed them that at least some of his bullets had found human lodging places.

Garvey had evidently succeeded in adding men to his gang, for more than a dozen gun flashes burst out at once. The attackers soon learned, however, that it wasn't healthy to attempt to rush the adobe. Surrounding it was impossible, and for a while they contented themselves with sending lead humming through the small window on the exposed side of the hut.

"We're in fo' a siege," Kid Wolf told the elder Robbins.

"Maybe we'd better give in to 'em," said the other.

Kid Wolf smiled and shook his head.

"That wouldn't save us. They'd butchah us, anyway. Nevah yuh worry. Before they get us, they'll find that The Wolf, from Texas, has teeth!"

"Then we'll play out the hand," agreed Robbins.

"To the last cahd," Kid Wolf drawled. "I have two hands heah that can turn up twelve lead aces to' a showdown. And I have anothah ace—a steel one, that's always in the deck."

The Texan saw as well as the others how desperate the situation had become. He knew that death would be the probable outcome for all of them.

Kid Wolf, however, was not a type of man who gave up. If they must go out, he decided, they would go out fighting.

The sun climbed the sky and disappeared over the distant blue range to the west, leaving the desert behind bathed in warm reds and soft purples. Then the shadows deepened, and night fell.

With it came a full moon, riding high out of the southeast—a pumpkin-colored, gigantic Arizona moon that changed to shining silver. Its light illuminated the scene and turned the landscape nearly as bright as day. This was a fact in favor of the three men cornered in the adobe. The attackers dared not show themselves in a rush. All night long their guns cracked, and they continued to do so when the east was beginning to lighten with the dawn.

Another day, and it proved to be one of torment.

There was no water. Before the hour of noon, the three besieged men were suffering from intense thirst. The little adobe was like an oven. The sun burned down pitilessly, distorting the air with waves of heat, and drawing mocking mirages in the sky. Bullets still hummed and buzzed about them. Every hissing slug seemed to whistle the mournful tune of "Death—death—death!" Late in the afternoon, the elder Robbins could endure the torture no longer.

"I'm goin' after water!" he cried.

Neither his son nor Kid Wolf could reason with him. He would not listen. He reasoned that although it was death to venture to the spring, it was also death to remain. He was nearly crazed with thirst.

"Let me go, then," said the Texan.

"No!" gasped Robbins. "Yuh stay with Dave. I'm old, anyway. Promise yuh'll stick with him, no matter what happens to me!"

"I promise," said The Kid, and the two men shook hands.

Getting to the water hole and back again was a forlorn hope, but Robbins was past reasoning. Lurching through the door, he ran outside the hut and toward the tulles. Young Robbins cried after his father, and then covered his eyes.

There was a sudden crackling of revolver fire. Spurts of bluish smoke blossomed out from the high grass—half a score of them! Bill Robbins staggered on his feet, reeled on a few steps, and then fell. His body had been riddled.

Kid Wolf's touch was tender as he took the orphaned youth's hand in his own. But his voice, when he spoke, was like his eyes—hard as steel:

"Garvey will join him, Dave, or we will! And if we do, let's hope we'll meet it as bravely. I have a plan. If we escape, we must do it tonight. Can yo' stick it out till then?"

Young Robbins nodded. The death of his father had been a great shock to him, but he did not flinch. In that desperate hour, Kid Wolf knew that he no longer had a boy at his side, but a man!

How the day wore its way through to a close was ever afterward a mystery to them. Their throats were parched, and their eyes bloodshot. To make matters worse, their horses, too, were suffering. Blizzard nickered softly from time to time, but quieted when Kid Wolf called to him through the wall.

Night brought some relief. Again the moon rose upon the tragic scene, and it grew cooler. Before the twilight had quite faded, Kid Wolf and Dave Robbins saw something that made them boil inwardly—the burial of Bill Robbins on Boot Hill!

Out of revolver range, a group of the bandits was filling up the grave. Garvey had made half of his threat good. And he was biding his time to complete his boast. The Texan's grave still waited!

A thin bank of clouds rolled up to obscure somewhat the light of the moon. This was what Kid Wolf had been waiting for. It was their only chance.

"I'm goin' to try and get through on foot," he whispered. "Befo' I go, I'll unloose Blizzahd. He's trained to follow, and he'll find me latah, if I make it. I don't dare ride him, because he's white and too good a tahget in the moon. I'll have to crawl toward Boot Hill. It's the only way out. In half an houah, yo' follow. Savvy?"

Dave nodded. Then The Kid added a few terse directions:

"I'll show yo' the way and meet yo' on the hill. Be as quiet and careful as an Indian, and take yo' time. If anything should happen to me, strike fo' yo' place on the San Simon. The reason I'm goin' first is so that yo' can escape in the excitement if they spot me. Heah's luck! I'll turn my hoss loose now."

They shook hands. Then, like a lithe moving shadow, the Texan crept out into the night.

CHAPTER XXIV

PURSUIT

Fire flames darted occasionally from the high tulles, licking the darkness like the tongues of venomous serpents. Rifles cracked, and bullets, fired at random, buzzed across the sand flats. Kid Wolf had an uncomfortable few minutes ahead of him.

Whenever the moon peeped out of its flying blanket of cloud, he was forced to lie flat and motionless on the ground. Lead often spattered uncomfortably close, but foot by foot he made his way toward Boot Hill.

This rise in ground, he believed, would be free from his enemies. After once reaching this, Dave Robbins and he would be on the road to safety. Blizzard, well trained, would follow him if he managed to elude the bullets of the Garvey gang.

The Texan was on Boot Hill now, and for the first time in many minutes, he breathed freely. The firing behind had become faint, and it was hardly likely that any watchers remained on the hill.

But Kid Wolf received a thrill of horror and surprise. The moon drifted free of its cloud curtain for a moment. He was standing not a dozen feet from the two freshly made graves. One, with Bill Robbins' headboard over it, was covered with a mound of earth.

Standing near the other, with a cocked revolver in his hand, was the half-breed, Charley Hood! His cruel lips were parted in a terrible smile as he slowly raised the weapon to a level with his eyes!

While Kid Wolf had been creeping toward Boot Hill, Dave Robbins was in the adobe hut, counting the dragging minutes. The suspense, now that the time for action was at hand, was nerve-racking. Would the Texan make it? Robbins strained his ears for the triumphant yells that would announce The Kid's death or capture.

As the seconds grew to minutes, he began to breathe easier. When it seemed to him that a half hour had passed, he prepared to follow. The moon, however, was now too bright, and he had to wait fully a quarter of an hour more before the light faded to shadow again. When the moment arrived, he squirmed through the doorway and across the sands on his hands and knees.

Dave Robbins was frontier bred, and although his progress was slower than the Texan's had been, he crept along as silently as one of the redskins themselves. Not a mesquite twig snapped under his body; not a pebble rattled. It seemed to take him hours to reach the hill which Kid Wolf had pointed out to him. As he did so, the moonlight again became so bright that it made the landscape nearly as white as day. For a time, he lay flat against the ground; then he wriggled on.

Where was he? Would he find his friend, the Texan? He waited a while, and then whistled, soft and low. There was no answer. He looked around him, trying to decide where he was and what to do, His eyes fell upon the two recently dug graves. Headboards stood at each of them. Both were covered. Near the mounds lay a spade. The earth clinging to it was moist.

With his heart in his throat, Dave Robbins again looked at the grave markers. One read: "Bill Robbins." It was the grave of his father! The other mound was marked "Kid Wolf"!

For a few minutes, Dave Robbins stood numbed. Something terrible had happened; just what, he did not know. It seemed the end. Could his friend, the gallant Texan, have met death? It didn't seem possible, and yet the evidence was before his eyes. Anger against Garvey and his hired killers suddenly overcame him. A hot wave seemed to sweep over him. He turned about and faced, not the distant San Simon, but in the direction of his enemies.

"I'll get some of 'em before I go, Kid!" he cried.

As if in answer, something came to his ears that brought a cry of joy to the youth. It was a stanza of a familiar song, sung in the soft, musical accents of the South:

"Oh, bury me not on the lone prairie-ee!"

Turning about, Dave Robbins saw Kid Wolf's face in the moonlight! The shock of it left the youth weak for a moment. The two wrung hands, and Robbins blurted:

"I thought yuh were dead! What happened? Why this covered grave?"

"A half-breed lookout," the Texan explained in a whisper. "Ugly, but slow with a gun. He had the drop, so instead of reachin' fo' mah Colts, I pretended to raise mah hands. Then I gave him this—mah hole cahd, the thirteenth ace."

And Kid Wolf showed him the heavy bowie knife so carefully hidden in its sheath sewn to the inside of his shirt collar.

"With this through his throat, he fell right in the grave they'd dug fo' me. Then I saw the shovel, and I couldn't resist throwin' some dirt ovah him. Well, that's that. I hated to take his life, but I had to do it to save mine. The thing to do now is to get out of this."

"How do yuh expect yore hoss to get to us?" breathed Robbins.

"Listen." The Texan smiled. "He knows this call."

He waited for a lull in the rifle-popping below, and then he gave the coyote yell—a mournful cry that seemed to echo and reëcho. The sound was so perfect an imitation that Robbins could scarcely believe his ears. And it even fooled the Indians. It did not, however, deceive the sagacious horse that waited patiently in the adobe. The Kid clutched his young companion's arm. Straining their eyes, they saw a white something moving up an arroyo.

"That Blizzahd hoss is smahter than I am," chuckled the Texan. "He knows who his enemies are, and he knows how to keep out of their sight. Watch him climb that dry wash."

They held their breath until Blizzard, moving so noiselessly that his hoofs seemed as cushioned as a cougar's, reached the top of the hill. Then Kid Wolf led him over it and down again into a gully a little distance to the west of it. Ahead of them now was safety, if they could make it. The Texan mounted and swung up Robbins behind the saddle.

"Too bad we had to leave that twenty thousand, Kid," said Robbins.

The Kid's white teeth flashed in a smile.

"Really, Dave," he drawled, "do yo' think I'd let Garvey get away with that? That express box was just a blind. Don't yo' know what I did while the rest of yo' were tippin' back the stagecoach? No? Well, I transferred the twenty thousand to Blizzahd's saddle-bags, so the money"—he tapped the bulges on each

241

side of the big saddle—"is right heah!"

Kid Wolf, ever since he had taken charge of the express money, had realized his responsibility and trust. He would protect it with his life. If he could reach Mexican Tanks with it, the money would be safe, for a small post of soldiers and government scouts guarded the place.

They had not gone a half mile, however, when a sound of distant shouting broke out behind them.

"That means they've discovahed ouah absence," said the Texan, grimly. "We'll have ouah hands full befo' long!"

Robbins, and the Texan as well, had been through the country before, and knew the lay of the land. The former had learned the location of a water hole west of them in the hills, and they decided to head for that, as they were suffering from intense thirst. Blizzard, too, had not taken water for thirty-six hours.

The Apache is one of the best trailers in the world. They were under a terrible handicap, and both realized it. With the great white horse, strong as it was, carrying double, they could not hope to out-distance pursuit.

"Yuh'd better leave me, Kid," Robbins begged. "Befo' I'd leave yo'," returned the Texan, "I'd leave *me!*"

Dawn began to glow pink and orange behind them, and gradually the dim, star-studded vault overhead became gray with the new day. Shortly afterward, they reached the water hole. It was nearly dry, but enough moisture remained to refresh both horse and riders.

Then they went on again. Kid Wolf could tell by Blizzard's actions that they were being followed. Before long he himself saw signs. Little dust clouds began to show behind them, scattered over a line miles long.

"Garvey and his Apaches!" the Texan jerked out. "And they're gainin' fast."

"Can we beat 'em to Mexican Tanks?"

"No," The Kid drawled, "but we can fight!"

They soon saw the hopelessness of it all. The horizon behind them swarmed with moving dots—dots that grew larger and more distinct with every fleeting minute. Garvey had obtained reënforcements, without doubt, for there seemed to be no end to the pursuing Apaches.

Blizzard ran like the thoroughbred he was. But even his iron muscles could not stand the strain for long. The ponies behind were fresh, and the snow-white charger was tremendously handicapped with the added weight which had been placed upon it.

Puffs of white smoke blossomed out behind them. A bullet, spent and far short, dropped away to their left, sending up a geyser of sand.

"I guess we'll fight now," Kid Wolf said, drawing his six-guns.

The grim-faced fighter from Texas knew the ways of the Apaches and was prepared for what followed. It was not his first encounter with renegade red men of the Southwest. He was also aware of what awaited them if they were taken captive. Death with lead would be far more merciful.

The line of Apache warriors spread out even farther. Blizzard was speeding over a flat table-land now, flanked by two ridges of iron-gray hills. A file of Indians separated from the main body and raced along the left-hand ridge. Another file of copper-brown, half-naked savages drummed along to the right.

Rifle fire crackled and flashed. Bullets now began to buzz and whine like infuriated insects. Arrows, falling far short, whistled an angry tune. The Kid held his fire and bade Dave Robbins follow his example. It was no time to waste lead.

"Go, Blizzahd, like yo' nevah went befo'!" cried the Texan.

The beautiful white horse seemed to realize its master's danger. It ran on courage alone. Its nostrils were expanded wide, its flanks and neck foam-flecked. The steel muscles rippled under its snowy hide, until it seemed to fly like a winged thing. But it is one thing to carry a hundred and sixty pounds; another thing to bear nearly three hundred. The pace could not last.

Kid Wolf pinned his hopes on reaching a deep arroyo ahead of them. Already the range was becoming deadly. A bullet ripped through the Texan's hat. Another burned his side. Directly behind them, Garvey and his gunmen—the two Arnolds, Henry Shank, and Stephenson—pounded furiously, gaining at every jump. Their mounts were better than those of the Indians, and Kid Wolf saw that they must be stopped at all costs.

For the first time, his guns belched flame. The two

Arnolds went down, unhorsed. Even in that desperate moment, Kid Wolf hesitated to kill until it was necessary. The Arnolds, however, were out of the chase for good and all. Stephenson also felt the crippling sting of the Texan's lead and toppled from his mount, drilled high in the shoulder.

Henry Shank and Gil Garvey, shaken at The Kid's marksmanship, drew in their horses, unwilling to press closer. That gave Blizzard his chance to make the shelter of the arroyo. Suddenly it yawned at their feet—a terrific jump. Would Blizzard take it? A reassuring pressure of a knee was all the inspiration the horse needed. They seemed to rush through the air. Then they were sliding down the bank in a cloud of dust, Blizzard tense and stiff-legged. By a miracle, they reached the bottom unhurt, and without losing a second, Kid Wolf headed his faithful mount into a thick paloverde clump.

"We'll have to stand 'em off heah," he panted.

The Texan's eyes surveyed his exhausted horse. They seemed to light with an idea. Even in that desperate plight, his mind worked rapidly.

"I've got a hunch, Dave," he said. "It may not help us, but—"

He quickly loaded one of his .45s and stuck it down in one of Blizzard's stirrups in such a way that it could not jolt out. Then he gave the horse a sharp pat on the neck.

"Go, Blizzahd," he urged, "until I call!"

The horse seemed to understand perfectly, for it

wheeled and ran with all its speed down the arroyo. It was soon lost to sight among the mesquites.

"He'll stay out of sight and within call," explained the Texan. "We may need him worse than we do now. Anyway, Garvey will have plenty trouble gettin' that express money."

They prepared to fight it out until the last, for already the Indians were forcing their ponies down into the arroyo. A triumphant shout went up—a shout that became an elated, bloodthirsty war cry. The Apaches saw that the two white men were almost within their grasp.

"Good-by, Dave," said The Kid.

They grasped hands for a moment. There was no fear in their faces. Then they confronted the renegades. It was to be their last stand!

"Here's hopin' we get Garvey before we go!" said Robbins fiercely.

A storm of bullets tore through the paloverdes, sending twigs and leaves flying. Kid Wolf smiled coolly along the barrel of his remaining gun, and he deliberately lined the sights.

The impact of the explosions kicked the heavy weapon about in his hand, but every shot brought grief to some savage. Robbins' gun also blazed.

A half dozen screaming Apaches rushed their position in the thicket. The charge failed, stopped by lead. Another came, almost in the same breath. It faltered, then came on, reënforced. There were too many of them for two men to check.

Kid Wolf understood their guttural cries as they advanced.

"They mean to take us alive!" he cried. "Don't let 'em do it, son! It's better to die fightin'!"

But the Apaches seemed to have more than an ordinary reason for wanting to capture them. They came on, a coppery swarm, clubbing their guns.

There was no time to reload! The two young white men found themselves fighting hand to hand in desperate battle. Kid Wolf smashed two of the Indians, sending them sprawling back into their companions with broken heads. But still they came—dozens of them!

Robbins was down, then up again. He felt hands seize him. Kid Wolf felt the impact of a gun stock on his head. The world seemed to sway crazily. Even while falling to the ground he still fought, his hard fists landing on the faces and chests of the red warriors in smashing blows. His feet were seized, then one arm. In vain he tried to tear himself loose.

"Fine! Now throw some rope around 'em!" they heard Garvey say.

A shower of blows fell upon the Texan's head. He dropped, with a half dozen red warriors clinging to him. It was the end!

CHAPTER XXV

BLIZZARD'S CHARGE

K id Wolf was so dazed for a time that he but dimly realized what was happening to him. Half stunned, he was carried, along with Dave Robbins, out of the arroyo. He was light-headed from the blows he had received.

That torture was in store for them, he well knew. He heard Gil Garvey's voice calling for Yellow Skull. Red faces, smeared with war paint, glared at him. He was being taken on a pony's back through a thicket of brush.

They were up on the mesa again, for he felt the sun burn out and a hot wind sweep the desert. What were they waiting for?

Yellow Skull! Kid Wolf had heard of that terrible, insane Apache chief. He could expect about as much mercy from him as he could from Garvey.

Some one was shaking his shoulder. It was the Lost Springs bandit leader.

Kid Wolf looked about him. A score or more of warriors, naked save for breechcloths, stood around in a hostile circle. Garvey was chuckling and in high good humor. With him was Shank, sneering and cold-eyed.

"We want to know where that money is!" Garvey shouted.

Kid Wolf's brain was clearing. On the ground, a few feet away, lay Dave Robbins, still stunned.

"I'm not sayin'," the Texan returned calmly.

Garvey's blotched face was convulsed with rage.

"Yuh'll wish yuh had, blast yuh!" he snarled. "I'm turnin' yuh both over to Yellow Skull! He's got somethin' in store for yuh that'll make yuh wish yuh'd never been born! Yo're west o' the Pecos now, Mr. Wolf—and there's no law here but me!"

The Kid eyed him steadily. "Theah's no law," he said, "but justice. And some of these times, sah, yo' will meet up with it!"

"I suppose yuh think yuh can hand it to me yoreself," leered the bandit leader.

"I may," said Kid Wolf quietly.

Garvey laughed loudly and contemptuously.

"Yellow Skull!" he called. "Come here!"

The man who strode forward with snakelike, noiseless steps was horrible, if ever a man was horrible. He was the chief of the renegade Apache band, and as insane as a horse that has eaten of the loco weed. Sixty years or more in age, his face was wrinkled in yellow folds over his gaunt visage. Above his beaked nose, his beady black eyes glittered wickedly, and his jagged fangs protruded through his animal lips. He wore a breechcloth of dirty white, and his chest was naked, save for two objects—objects terrible enough to send a thrill of horror through the beholder. Suspended on a long cord around his neck were two shriveled human hands. Above this was a necklace made of dried human fingers.

"Yellow Skull," said Garvey, pointing to Kid Wolf,

249

"meet the man who slew yore son, Bear Claw!"

The expression of the chief's face became ghastly. His eyes widened until they showed rings of white; his nostrils expanded. With a fierce yell, he thumped his scrawny chest until it boomed like an Indian drum. Then he gave a series of guttural orders to his followers.

Kid Wolf, who knew the Apache tongue, listened and understood. His sunburned face paled a bit, but his eyes remained steady. He turned his head to look at Robbins, who was recovering consciousness.

"Keep up yo' nerve, son," he comforted. "I'm afraid this is goin' to be pretty terrible."

The bonds of the two white men were loosened, and they were pulled to their feet and made to walk for some distance. Garvey and Shank, grinning evilly, accompanied them.

Kid Wolf felt the comforting weight of his hidden knife at the back of his neck. It would do him little good, however, to draw it, for he was hemmed in by the Apaches. He might get two or three, but in the end he would be beaten down. He was determined, at any rate, to go out fighting. If he could only bring justice to Garvey before he died, he would be content. Tensely he waited for the opportune time.

One of the redskins carried a comb of honey. The Texan knew what that meant. The most horrible torture that could have been devised by men awaited them.

The torture party paused in a clear space in the middle of a high thicket of mesquite. Here in the sun-baked, packed sand were two ant hills.

Kid Wolf had heard of the method before. What Yellow Skull intended to do was this: The two prisoners would be staked and tied so tightly over the ant hills that neither could move a muscle. Then their mouths would be propped open and honey smeared inside. The swarming colonies of red ants would do the rest.

For the first time, Dave Robbins seemed to realize what was in store for them. He turned his face to the Texan's, his eyes piteous.

"Kid!" he gasped, horrified.

"Steady, son," said Kid Wolf. "Steady!"

Quick hope had suddenly begun to beat in his breast. Deep within the mesquite thicket, he had caught sight of something white and moving. It was his horse! Blizzard had followed his master, and stood ready to do his bidding.

Already the grinning Apaches were coming forward with the stakes and ropes. Not a second was to be lost. It was a forlorn hope, but Kid Wolf knew that he could depend on Blizzard to do his best. Sharp and clear, the Texan gave the coyote yell!

"Yip-yip-ee!"

What happened took place so suddenly that the Apaches never realized what it all was! *Crash!* Like a white, avenging ghost horse, the superb Texas charger leaped out of the mesquite, muscles bunched. It made the distance to its master's side in two flashing leaps, bowling over a half dozen Indians as it did so! The Apaches fell back, overcome with astonishment.

With a quick movement, Kid Wolf drew his knife, pulling it from his neck sheath like lightning. With it he felled the nearest warrior. Another step brought him to Blizzard's side.

Garvey and Shank, acting quicker than their red allies, drew their revolvers.

"Get him! Shoot 'em down!" they yelled.

But Kid Wolf had seized the gun he had placed in Blizzard's stirrup. He dropped to his knees to the sand, just as lead hummed over his head.

Dave Robbins had struck one of the amazed Apaches and had jerked his rifle away from him. Clubbing it, he smashed two others as fast as they dived in.

Shank rushed, his gun winking spurts of fire.

Kid Wolf could not spare his enemies now. His own life depended on his flashing Colt. He lined the tip of his front sight and thumbed the hammer.

Thr-r-r-rup! Shank gasped, as lead tore through him. He dropped headfirst, arms outstretched.

"Get on the hoss!" The Kid yelled at Robbins. Then he turned his gun on Garvey.

In his rage, the Lost Springs desperado fired too quickly. His aim was bad, and the slug sang over the Texan's head.

"Reckon yo' are about to get the law that's west of the Pecos now, Garvey—justice!"

With his words, The Kid threw down on Garvey and suddenly snapped the hammer. The bullet found its mark. If Garvey had no heart, Kid Wolf's bullet found the spot where it ought to be. With his glazing eyes, Gil

252

Garvey—wholesale murderer—saw justice at last. Dropping his gun, he swayed for a moment on his feet, then fell heavily.

"Look out, Kid!" Robbins yelled.

The Texan whirled just in time. A pace behind him was Yellow Skull, his hideous face distorted with mad fury. In his thin hand was a long leather thong, to which was attached a round stone. A second more, and Kid Wolf's skull would have been smashed!

A burst of flame stopped him, The chief sagged, dropped. The Kid had fired just as the stone was whirled aloft. The Indians, now that their chief and white allies had fallen, retreated. The almost miraculous appearance of the horse had dismayed them and filled them with superstitious fear. A few more shots served to scatter them and send them flying for cover. Kid Wolf vaulted into the saddle. Robbins was already on Blizzard's back.

"Heads low!" sang out the Texan.

He headed the horse for the mesquites. Crashing through them, they found themselves on the mesa plain once more. Kid Wolf urged Blizzard to greater speed. Bullets buzzed around them, but it was evident that the Apaches had lost heart. Blizzard pounded on, and the cries behind soon grew fainter and fainter. Kid Wolf relaxed a little and grinned.

"That's what I'd call a narrow squeak," he chuckled. "How far to Mexican Tanks?"

"On over the mesa," panted Robbins, "five or six miles."

"Then we'll make it," decided The Kid.

A quarter of an hour later, they drew rein and looked behind. Whether the Indians feared to approach any nearer to the government post, or whether they had given up through superstitious fear, would have been hard to tell. At any rate, there was nothing to be seen of them.

Two miles below the two men could see the little post known as Mexican Tanks, scattered out in a fertile, cottonwood-grown valley. With one accord, they shook hands.

"Now will yo' believe me," asked the Texan, "when I tell yo' that Blizzahd's a smaht hoss?"

Dave Robbins grinned. "So's his master," he chuckled. "And speakin' o' Blizzard again, I guess we owe him some water and a peck of oats. Reckon we'll find it down there." His face sobered. "It won't do me any good, Kid, to thank yuh."

"Don't try," drawled The Kid. "I'm a soldier of misfohtune, and excitement's mah business. I'll leave yo' down heah, son. Go to yo' claim on the San Simon and make good—fo' yo' fathah's sake. And good luck!"

"Yuh won't come along?"

Kid Wolf shook his head and smiled.

"I'm just a rollin' stone," he confessed, "and I just naturally roll toward trouble. If yo' evah need me again, yo'll find me where the lead flies thickest. As soon as I turn this express money ovah to the authorities, I'll be on my way again. Maybe it'll be the Rio Grande, perhaps the Chisholm Trail, and maybe—

254

well, maybe I'll stay west of the Pecos and see what I can see. Quién sabe?"

Blizzard cocked his ears and turned his head to look his master in the eye. Blizzard savvied. He was "in the know."

Center Point Publishing
600 Brooks Road ● PO Box 1
Thorndike ME 04986-0001 USA

(207) 568-3717

US & Canada:
1 800 929-9108